Acknowledgements:

Thank you to my Beta Readers from my online writing group:

Jjstar, Rob Caudle, Stalking Wolf, October 21, adewpearl, robina1978, Norbanus, heyjude, alexisleech, Mrs. Dark, Writingfundimension, Dutchie, robyn corum, mommerry, Fleedleflump, nancyjam, squid152, Adele Symonds, forestport12, emmex, Curtis Hatch, barking dog, dejohnsrld, nor84, Mr. Green, Louisiana Poorboy, Peter@Poole, mtrybank, Maureen Napier, JM daSilva, Yezall, Gungalo, Dan Hafertepe, Honeycomb, EricDaGoose, Mastery, Rondeno, Phyllis Stewart, Perp Ihebom, Edward M. Baldwin, Amandastory, hollyinvesuvianite, unimatrix001, Slythytove2, Carmanie Bhatti, rgabel, Beverley101, Irmoses4, emmex, visionary1234, justatuna, turtledove, Titus, Aaron James, David Graham

Thank you to my poetry and SPAG teacher, Brooke Baldwin.
Thank you to my online writing group, FanStory.com

Thank you to my mother-in-law, Nancy Graham;
First reader and advisor

Thank you to Doug Evans
for the cover photo

Thank you to Murray Graham for advice.

Thank you to Sarah J. King-D'Souza, Q.C. for advice

Thank you to Breanne, Matt, Scott, Hollie, Mike, Simone, Keaton, and Mason

Dedicated to my wonderful husband and best friend,
David Graham
For showing me that I can reach for the stars
and achieve my dreams.

In loving memory of my brother,
Wayne Sidney Bernard Buan
August 15, 1949 – December 4, 2011

Chapter 1

The Letter

Carly Davenport stood shivering in the freezing cold, holding the door open. She tried to make out the smudged return address on the envelope she just received. It must be important, to be delivered by courier. The address, to her husband Sam, was clear enough, but the smeared return address was hard to read. She squinted, stared and studied.

"Sam doesn't know anyone in Russia."

She thanked the courier, closed the door, climbed the stairs, hesitantly placed the envelope on the desk and went back into the kitchen to continue preparing supper. She opened the oven door to check on the roasting chicken. It was browning nicely. She washed the vegetables for the salad and began to chop them up. Carly did not enjoy eating salad, but the doctor told her she had to eat better now that her cholesterol was high.

When she finished with the salad, she set the table. Thursdays were a rush dinner because Sam had a guys' night out with his old military buddies. She wasn't quite sure what they did on Thursday nights but she never questioned Sam. He had always been a faithful breadwinner for the family, and Carly respected his one night out a week. Still, she couldn't help dreaming of enticing him to stay home with a bubble bath in the candlelight.

Finished setting out the plates and cutlery, she walked through the living room and caught a glimpse of the letter again. It was as if the thing was calling to her to open it. She couldn't possibly invade her husband's privacy by opening his mail. Or could she? She picked the envelope up and turned it over a few times. It was fairly heavy. They used a big square envelope that could hold a Christmas card. It was thick like it had a stack of pictures inside. She shook her head and put the envelope down. It wouldn't be right

and she, Carly Savannah Davenport, would not open someone else's mail.

She placed a jug of ice water in the fridge to keep it cold until Sam came home from work. With everything pretty much ready, she sat down in front of the television and began clicking through the channels. A cooking show caught her attention. They were discussing chocolate recipes. Carly loved chocolate and was having a terrible time toning down her diet because of her cholesterol issues.

Her eyes were glued to the TV screen as they showed the picture of the triple-chocolate cheesecake they were preparing to make. They pulled out a springform pan and Carly knew she had one of those just begging to be used in her kitchen cupboards. She quickly ran to the desk to get paper and a pen to make notes. She was so going to try this recipe.

There was that letter looking at her again. She was going to hand it to Sam the minute he walked in the door and watch him open it. That letter was just about driving her crazy with curiosity. Maybe some long lost relative had died and left all his millions to Sam. She heaved a big sigh and told herself to stop thinking such fantastic thoughts.

She and Sam were average folks and luxuries were not in their future. They were perfectly happy with the life they chose. They started their family soon after they were married. They wanted babies right away. Then everyone said it's best to have all your babies at the same time so you get through the diaper stage all at once. Three beautiful babies later they were a busy family on a tight budget. While everyone else on their street seemed to have two cars and a boat, they could only imagine what those luxuries might be like. They might have been cash strapped most of the time but they wouldn't have wanted it any other way. Their children brought them happiness beyond measure. When Sam was away in the military so much, the children kept Carly company. There's nothing better than having your five year old pat you on the back and say *it's ok mommy, Daddy will be back soon to take care of us*. Now that the kids were grown up and living on their own, Carly was having trouble remembering the exact way her five year old said those comforting words all those years ago. Hugs and kisses from her babies was the best reward Carly could have ever asked for.

Carly picked up the picture of her children and grandchildren. Kristy, the oldest, was sitting on the floor holding two month old baby Cooper while eight year old Claire was snuggled up to her Auntie. Emma was sitting on the floor with four year old Curtis cuddled up in her lap. Caleb was sitting on a chair behind his two sisters. Carly just loved that picture. Each time she looked at it she was amazed at how time had gone by for her children to grow up into such fine adults. Emma was the youngest but she was the first to marry and have children. Kristy got her University degree and was teaching music. Caleb was going to school and working as an Electrician's apprentice.

The TV program brought Carly back to the present and she was upset with herself that they were now putting the finishing touches on the triple-chocolate cheesecake. It looked so delicious and Carly's mouth watered as the hostess and her guest took their first bite of the mound of chocolate.

Chapter 2

Guests for Dinner

Disappointed that she didn't get to see them making the triple-chocolate cheesecake, Carly pouted while she grabbed the remote and started flipping through the channels. She found one of her favorite talk shows and decided to watch that while she waited for Sam to come home. The topic of the show was the Empty Nest Syndrome. Carly could certainly relate to that subject. She was living it. The kids moved out one by one. Then one would return home and leave again. Carly had to admit that she missed her kids a lot. The house was so empty, she could hear the clocks ticking.

The phone rang and Carly jumped. It startled her but when she saw it was Emma she answered it right away.

"Hello," she said tucking her brown tresses behind her ear.

"Hi Mom, whatcha doing?" Emma asked.

"Watching TV while I wait for your father to come home from work."

"Oh, I see."

"Why, what are you up to? You sound like you're on your cell phone."

"Yeah, I got the kids in the car and we are thinking of coming over to see you. If that's OK."

"I hope you aren't driving while you're on the phone."

"No, we're just sitting in the driveway. We haven't left yet. The kids wanted to know if they can come over to your house, for a sleepover."

"Oh sure. That would be fine. Your dad has his night out with the boys tonight so the kids would be good company for me."

"Great!" Emma's enthusiasm came over the phone loud and clear. "Cooper too? I could use a night of actual sleep."

"Sure," Carly smiled. "The more the merrier."

"What's for supper?"

"I have a chicken roasting in the oven and I made a salad. What can I make for the kids?"

"I'll stop at the grocery store on the way over and pick something up. Do you want me to get anything for you while I'm there?" Emma asked.

"Hmmm, let me think, maybe a fresh fruit tray and some cookies. Oh, and get some chocolate milk because Curtis really likes to drink that now."

"OK, I'll be there in about twenty minutes. See you soon."

Carly hung up the phone and went to the pantry to get a package of macaroni and cheese. If all else fails, the kids will eat that. Claire was easy enough to feed because she'd eat pretty much everything. Curtis was the fussy one.

Twenty minutes later, Emma pulled up in front of the house and parked on the street. Carly's heart always skipped a beat when the kids arrived for a visit. The grandchildren meant the world to her. Curtis was always the first one to come running to the door after his mom let him out of the truck.

"Grandma," he called. "We got you a plant. The pot is bla-lue." He held it carefully in his hands as he ran up the steps to the house.

Carly stepped forward to take the plant from him before he dropped it. She giggled to herself that her four year old grandson never slowed down. "Thank you, it's lovely."

"Welcome," Curtis sang as he went inside the house, kicked his boots off, dropped his jacket on the floor and ran up the stairs to check out the movie selection. Carly followed him up the stairs and placed the potted plant on the desk beside the letter, then returned to the front door.

"Hi, Honey!" Carly cried as her granddaughter gave her a big squeezy hug. Then, with the baby carrier safely on Carly's arm, they all went inside where it was warm.

"Chicken smells good, momma," Emma said. "I have to go back out to the truck and get the groceries. I'll be right back."

Carly settled the baby carrier on the floor in the living room and admired the sleeping baby before turning her attention to Curtis and Claire. "Is everyone hungry?"

"Yes," Claire answered. "I'm starving."

"I not hungry," Curtis answered. "My tummy's full."

"Well, what have you been eating that your tummy is so full?" Carly asked.

"Oh, he had some cereal in the car," Claire answered for him. "Mommy says he has to eat some supper though."

"Everyone has to eat a no thank you helping at my table. You'll have a tiny piece of chicken, a tiny bit of salad, and a tiny bit of macaroni."

"Oh, I like mackeonies," Curtis piped up. "With ketchups."

"I think we can arrange that," Carly smiled as she walked into the kitchen to add more plates to the table. The kids had their own special plates and cutlery that she kept just for them.

Emma brought the groceries in to the kitchen and helped get the supper ready. "When will Dad be home?"

"Oh, anytime now," Carly replied looking at the clock. "I bet if the kids went to the door they might see his truck pull into the driveway."

Curtis flew to the door to wait for Grandpa. "He's here, he's here! Grandpa, we got Grandma a flower at the store. Can we play the batman game?"

Sam managed to get inside the door before Curtis threw himself into his arms and gave him a great big hug. "I love you Grandpa!"

"Hi Grandpa!" Claire called as she followed Sam into the living room. "We're here for a sleepover."

Sam bent down to pick up the sleeping Cooper and cradle him in his arms. "We're staying for supper!" Curtis piped up. "I get to eat mackeonies with ketchups!"

"That's great news, buddy!" Sam ruffled Curtis's hair and sat down to enjoy his time with his grandchildren. Claire put the game into the machine and Curtis grabbed the controls. "I want a turn to play but I don't know how."

"I'll show you," said Claire. Curtis was content to stand and watch as Claire played the level. Curtis gave instructions to her but she quietly played it her own way. Grandpa gave advice when needed and they all focused on playing the game together.

"OK, supper's ready," Emma called from the dining room. "My two little buddies need to come and sit at the table."

"I want Grandpa to sit beside me," shouted Curtis as he ran to his seat at the table.

"I want Grandma to sit beside me," echoed Claire.

Everyone chattered while they ate. Curtis ate all his macaroni but left the tiny portions of chicken and salad. He drank his chocolate milk and asked for more. Claire ate everything on her plate and had seconds as well.

"That was a great supper, honey," Sam said as he got up to put his dishes in the sink. I have to go now because the boys will be wondering where I am.

"But, Dad," Emma interrupted. "I brought dessert. Aren't you going to have some?"

"Ohh, I can't. I really have to go now."

Before they knew what was happening, Sam had grabbed his coat and flown out the door. They heard the truck tires squeal as he backed out of the driveway and drove away.

Stunned, Carly broke the silence by asking, "Who wants ice cream?"

Once the dishes were all taken off the table and loaded into the dishwasher, Emma announced that she was going to go home. Carly had the baby in her arms as she waved good bye to Emma. Carly always made Claire and Curtis stand at the window and wave good bye to their mother. It took great effort to get Curtis into that habit because he wanted to get busy with playing at Grandma's house.

"It's my turn to pick a movie," Curtis hollered as he ran gleefully to the cupboard. Claire looked annoyed but she knew it would be her turn to choose once Curtis's movie was over. "Toy Wars!" Claire and Carly looked at each other and groaned. It would be the umpteenth time that they watched that movie. They practically knew every word before the characters said it.

"Claire," Carly asked. "Can you bring me the baby's bottle?"

Carly watched Claire run to the diaper bag and get the bottle. That's when she noticed the letter was not on the desk.

Darn! She thought to herself. *I wanted to see Sam open that letter*.

"Thanks luv," she said to Claire and they all settled in to watch the movie.

Chapter 3

Operation Walls of Jericho

The letter sitting on the desk, addressed to Sam, had caught his attention immediately as he came in the house. He tucked it into his pocket when nobody was looking. He did his best to keep everyone talking during dinner so he would not have to answer any questions. As soon as he finished eating, he excused himself and practically ran for the door. Once he drove far enough away from the house, he pulled the truck over to read the letter.

He immediately pulled out his cell phone and called the team lead. His breath could be seen as he spoke due to the chilly November weather.

"Change of location. Operation Walls of Jericho is now in effect. Do a fan out."

Sam went to headquarters, the hangar where he worked. He was not retired from the military like Carly thought. It was all a ruse because he was actually sent into top secret undercover duties. Wives were not allowed to know this information. The hangar appeared to be a civilian aviation company but it was really an active military facility.

Heading into the hangar through the pilot door, he made his way to the briefing room. The rest of the team arrived shortly after Sam did. They all knew this mission was about to go live, they just didn't know when or how. The initial call alerted the team leader, Brian Grant, to call all team members to assemble immediately. They all knew the code and exactly what they were expected to do.

There was no talking as everyone took a seat in the plush black leather chairs situated around the large table. The door was locked once everyone was in attendance. The room was sound proofed and de-bugged, so it was shielded from all electronic intelligence gathering devices.

Standing before the group, he popped a thumb drive into the slide projector and began the presentation.

"A package from Agent Archie, in Russia, arrived at my residence today. He has reason to believe his cover has been exposed and he's in imminent danger. He broke protocol by sending it to my house, so we know the situation had to be dire. We have not heard from Archie for over a week now. It is assumed he has perished. We now have in our possession photos and videos to prove that Thor's Hammer has been stolen by a terrorist group. Their intent is to bomb an unknown location filled with civilian innocents. We must get the information to Commander Steele immediately. We have trained for this; you all know your roles."

A slide show presentation allowed the team to see shots of suspected terrorists and key players as well as shots of the top secret Thor's Hammer before it was stolen. Sam knew his team members would store these images in their memories. This was their only opportunity to view the information. They could not risk being caught with any kind of a paper trail. These highly trained individuals knew the dangers of being caught by the enemy.

"Sir," called out Rick Baker. "We can have the jet ready for you tomorrow morning. Boots on the tarmac at 0500 hours, wheels up at 0600."

"Your parachute will be ready and waiting for you, sir," reported Graham Marsden. "It will be a HAHO jump. High Altitude High Open. All updates and modifications are complete. You'll have all the latest technology at your fingertips when you jump."

"The alterations to the jet have been completed. The HAHO door in the belly of the fuselage is now operational, sir. I finished final touches last night. You can jump out of the aircraft safely without being sucked into the engines," reported Jim Kingswell.

"I have one SNAFU that I need help with," Sam told the group. "As you all know, Archie sent the package to my house. My wife accepted the package and signed for it. They could target her as a way to get at me. Her safety is in jeopardy."

"Oh," the group buzzed in conversation as they looked at each other in bewilderment. Jessica spoke up, "we can take her with us and make her think she is on a routine holiday."

The group mumbled some more conversations and everyone laughed nervously.

"That's not a bad idea," replied Sam. "Can the team keep her busy shopping or something?"

"I don't know about shopping, sir. We have our own duties to focus on. We'll come up with a plan by tomorrow morning. Don't you worry."

"Any ideas how I'm going to get my wife on the plane?" Silence filled the room. Sam got the message. He knew he'd have to do some fast thinking of his own. "All right then. I'll come up with something. You all better be prepared to play along with the charade when I bring her here tomorrow morning. I don't want her to see any of our equipment due to the secrecy required for this mission. I am counting on all of you to keep her safe when I am gone. I look forward to seeing how you handle that! Get your affairs in order before morning, ladies and gentlemen. You know the dangers involved in this mission. Dismissed."

****

Sam sat in his truck and phoned his son-in-law, Ethan. The grand-kids needed to be picked up very early. It would be sudden and had to be handled smoothly without drama. Ethan had to be told there was concern for the family's safety. Ethan, being a police officer, would know how to handle the situation at his end. Sam trusted him and knew he would understand the nature of this mission without requiring too many details.

****

It was 2:00 am when Sam finally got home. He tiptoed quietly into the master bedroom. Carly was sleeping peacefully. He paused to admire his wife. He loved her soft curly brown hair and the way it was sprawled out on the pillow. She was his whole world and he couldn't bear it if anything were to happen to her. The team would stop at nothing to keep her safe. He knew he could focus on his own mission without worrying. He was trained to get the job done, and he would do nothing less. He had a duty to his country. He knew his wife would be proud of him when the mission was successfully completed.

He regretted that he had to lie to Carly about retiring from the military. He was certain he would have a lot of explaining to do. She was well aware of the secrecy involved in his work, but that was before she thought he retired. He would deal with that later. For now, work came first. Maybe after this mission he would consider retiring for real.

The baby squirmed and grunted in the travel bassinet beside the bed. Sam peeked in and saw that little Cooper had his blue eyes open wide like glowing beacons in the night. He scooped the baby up in his arms and took him to the living room to inspect his diaper. He didn't want to disturb Carly's sleep. She was likely exhausted from babysitting the three grandchildren all by herself. Mostly he wanted her to be rested for the trip she didn't yet know about. He would allow her to have two more hours of sleep. They had to be on that airplane by 0500 dark and dirty.

Cooper cooed while Sam removed the diaper. "This is one wet package you're wearing, little man. Let Grandpa get you changed. We'll let Grandma sleep."

Chapter 4

Boarding Pass

It was dark when Carly felt Sam crawl into bed. He snuggled under the covers and gave her a peck on the cheek. "Hey babe," he whispered, and then kissed her on the lips.

Carly opened one eye and peeked at him. He planted several little kisses on each cheek and her forehead. Carly opened both eyes and wondered what this was all about. He then gave her a warm and passionate kiss.

"What's going on?" she asked.

"I just wanted to kiss my beautiful wife."

"Have you been drinking?" she asked suspiciously.

"Nope, just passionately in love with my wife of 30 years is all."

"Wow, I like that." She snuggled in and rested her head on his chest.

"I have a surprise for you. Are you interested in being spoiled?"

"Of course I am. I love being spoiled."

"Honey." He hesitated a moment then blurted, "Honey, we bought an airplane!"

"You what? Is this some kind of joke? You have been drinking. We don't have the money to buy an airplane. Stop kidding me, I better check on the baby. He slept through the night like a good boy." She turned to check the bassinet but there was no baby in it. "Where's the baby?"

"Ethan came to get the kids about twenty minutes ago. We got them to the car as quiet as we could. We didn't want to wake you."

"Why on earth would Ethan come to get the kids at such an ungodly time in the morning?" Carly looked at the clock, "It's 4:00 am. What's going on, Sam?"

"Well, I bought an airplane. It was a junker and me and the guys wanted to see if we could fix it up and get it flight worthy. That's what we've been doing every Thursday for the last couple of months. A real labor of love, I'm telling you. We still have the skills we were taught in the military. Sarge would be proud of us."

"How much did you pay for it?"

"Oh, it was a steal. We split the cost. Only a couple a hundred bucks each," he lied convincingly. *More like $5 million before all the multimillion dollar high tech upgrades the military needs, he thought to himself.* "Boss said we could keep it at the hangar. Besides, we plan to sell it later and make a profit."

"How come you didn't tell me about it?"

"I wanted to surprise you. Anyway, it's ready now. We did a great job on it. You'd never know it was a clunker. It looks almost brand new."

"Wow, that sounds awesome, Sam."

"Oh yeah, it's awesome all right," Sam was getting into this lie. He almost scared himself at how convincing he sounded. She didn't have to know the plane actually belonged to the military. "So, I want to take you away for the weekend. We could fly to Las Vegas. It'll be fun. Just you and me." To enhance his acting skills, he took Carly in his arms and gave her another passionate kiss. Then he held her like it was the last hug he would have in a long time.

"Wow! You are pretty proud of your airplane. I almost think you're planning for us to join the mile high club. Now that would be something," she giggled. "What time do we leave?"

"In fifteen minutes. Do you think you can shower and be ready by then? The cab is on its way to take us to the airport."

"Wha, what? Seriously? Oh my gawd, Sam. Why the rush?"

"I had to submit a flight plan and that was the time they said they had available for takeoff," he lied again.

"You filed a flight plan. Who exactly is going to fly this plane?"

"I am. Sam Davenport, pilot at your service."

"When did you learn to fly an airplane? You are full of stories all of a sudden."

"Oh, when we worked on the planes in the military they let us try flying once in a while. After all, we had to know how to park the planes. Sometimes one of us technicians had to sit in the pilot seat to steer in the right direction." The bullshit meter was rising with every word coming out of Sam's mouth.

"Wow, I didn't know that."

"Yeah," he stood her up and walked her to the washroom. "Get in that shower and get ready." He playfully slapped her on the bottom. "Time is a ticking. Actually, since the pilot can't join the mile high club, I thought maybe you could help me earn my boarding pass." He grinned and chased her into the shower.

****

Thirty minutes later they climbed out of the cab in front of the hangar. They were a little behind schedule but Sam thought it was worth it to make love to his wife once more before their long separation. He was pleased with the steamy memory he would have of her.

The large blue hangar was lit up like a Christmas tree in the dark. They walked through the front business entrance to the office area. The technicians were in their dirty white coveralls, standing around drinking coffee. They turned to say "Good morning," to Sam and Carly. "Plane's ready for you, boss."

"Oh, Carly, I forgot to mention that our crew of Daves is going to be flying with us. They helped renovate the old junker plane up so's the least we can do is all have the first flight together."

Carly raised an eyebrow but didn't protest. "Okay," she answered. So much for a romantic getaway, she thought to herself.

There were five guys that worked with Sam who all had the first name Dave. Sam was a joker and always made light of the fact. He affectionately called them the "*Dave crew*". He liked putting them on the same shift. If work needed to be done Sam would get on the loud speaker system and call "*Dave for plane recovery*". Then he'd giggle when they all came running at the same time to meet the incoming plane.

Carly also knew that Sam had a tendency to play around on the loud speaker system so they would occasionally ban him from making announcements. One of his favorite announcement jokes was to call "*Attention all shoppers, today's in store special is...*" The guys all thought it was funny, but management viewed it differently.

"So where is this fixed up plane of yours?" Carly asked.

Sam pointed out the window to the plane parked on the tarmac. "That's her right there, hon. You're gonna love her. Just wait till you see inside. The Dave crew did a great job of reupholstering the seats. I don't want to brag too much, but I rebuilt the engines myself."

Carly couldn't believe her eyes. She walked up to the observation window to get a better look. There it was in all its glory. A white private airplane. It had two wings, wheels, windows, and everything it would need in all the right places. There had to be a catch to this. Either that or the guys really did a great job of fixing it up.

The Dave crew crowded around Sam and Carly and did their best to beef up Sam's creative story. They weren't quite sure what exactly he told Carly but they thought they could puff up the glory of the jet.

"She's a 2005 Jet to Go. Painted her myself. White with royal blue trim. Once we reupholstered the interior seating, we had some spare time on our hands so we decided to change the tires too." Dave H rolled his eyes. *What a load of bull*, he thought to himself.

"Yeah," said Dave H wanting to outdo Dave J's expertise. "She's only got about 1,600 landings under her belt. Hardly been used at all. The tires weren't really in need of a change but we kinda like the old girl to have shiny tires. Gives off a better image if you know what I mean."

"Just wait till you hear her engines purr," added Dave H. "Nobody can do things to a jet engine like your Sam there." Then to add silliness to the charade he said, "I just hope I glued the wings on tight enough to survive the take off."

Dave N and Dave F stayed well behind Carly's line of vision trying their best to control their fits of giggles.

"Is there a washroom on that airplane?" Carly asked. "I could use a potty break right about now."

Dave H noticed the two giggling Daves and said, "Use the one down that hall and around the corner, Mrs. Davenport. Dave N and Dave F have a few free moments, they can point the way. We still have a bit of a wait before the jet is ready for boarding."

Carly thanked him and then she looked to the two Dave's. "I think I can find it by myself, guys. Thanks anyways." She gave Sam a private wink as she remembered his request to earn his boarding pass in the shower that morning.

Chapter 5

Ready for Takeoff

They climbed the stairs to the airplane. Carly could hardly contain her excitement. They turned to the right and stood there a moment. The walls were white and looked like any other plane she'd seen before, until she saw that the seats were all caramel color leather.

"Seats nine passengers," Sam explained. "The forward cabin has a four-place club with foldout tables. The aft cabin has a single club chair with foldout table opposite a three-place divan and a seat for a ninth passenger. The club chairs are covered in leather. There's drink compartments. We have a 15' LCD monitor. The cabin has video display system with cabin briefer. There is one DVD Player. The forward service area has a full-service galley with a microwave oven, coffee maker, cold storage unit, and lots of room for storage for dishes. The washroom is in the aft cabin. Dave F outdid himself when he finished the wood cabinetry in maple veneer. Dave N installed the brown carpet."

Carly listened to Sam mutter on with his description of the interior of the plane, but barely heard a word. She had never been inside a private airplane before and this moment took her breath away. This plane was much bigger than she imagined. She ran her hand along the leather seat and gently sat down. It was soft and comfy. She pulled the table out and put it away again. Then she leaned forward to look out the window.

"Everyone on board," Sam called out. The five Daves entered the plane. Dave Hall went into the little galley and came out with a cold glass of coke for Carly. "Here, drink this before we take off. These little private planes will make your ears pop something fierce. The drink will relax your ears so it won't be so bad. We're all used to it since servicing crews have to fly wherever the plane goes. We never know when it will need repairs on location."

Dave N handed a paper bag to Carly and said, "Use this if you feel sick. Some passengers feel airsick on a smaller plane."

"Seat belts on, we're ready to get started."

Sam pulled up the stairs and secured the door. Then he disappeared in the cockpit and closed the door behind him.

Carly watched everything going on around her with fascination. She still couldn't believe her husband was going to fly this airplane. She didn't know if she should be excited or terrified. She felt a sudden jerk of the airplane and then noticed they were moving. Looking out the small airplane window she could see the ground crew signaling to the pilot as the plane made its way towards the runway. They bumped along at a good pace until they came to a stop. They stayed still for a moment or two and then the plane turned onto the main runway. Carly could hear the sound of the engines roaring to life as they began to taxi down the runway.

Still in disbelief that her Sam was flying this plane, she wondered if they would actually lift off the ground. The force from the speed held her pressed back in her chair. She crossed herself, said a silent prayer, and closed her eyes. She could hear the tires stop moving on the ground and it felt smooth. They were airborne. This was all so fantastic to Carly.

She felt herself floating in the clouds and then drifting off to sleep.

****

Carly was dreaming that she was snoring. She could even hear someone snoring near her. She woke up with a start at the sound of a loud snorting snore. Her head had fallen back and her mouth was wide open. She was drooling and swiped at her mouth in embarrassment. Her brown leather carry on tote bag was looped around her shoulder and the bag rested on her lap.

When she looked around she was in a hotel lobby. Several people walked by and a few people were seated near her. There was a quiet hum of conversation and nobody seemed to be too concerned about Carly being there. She could hear a steady stream of water coming from the water fountain in the middle of the room. She hoped nobody had heard her snoring over the sound of the water.

How did I get here? Where's Sam? Where's the airplane?"

She stood up and headed straight to the nearest ladies room. She looked at herself in the mirror and was horrified. Her hair looked wind-blown; her mascara was running down her face. She examined her teeth and decided her breath was smelly. She dug through her tote bag and pulled out her toothbrush and toothpaste. After she brushed her teeth, she brushed her hair. Then she splashed water on her face so she could apply a fresh layer of makeup.

Once she got that out of the way she wandered around to see if she could find Sam. Maybe he was in the hotel restaurant. She walked toward the deserted restaurant and decided he wasn't there. She stepped outside and nodded to the man that held the door open for her. It was daylight outside and the weather was warm. It didn't look like she was in Las Vegas.

Carly felt lightheaded and needed to sit down. She found a bench and barely got to it on time before her legs gave out. She sat there a while until she felt strong enough to get up again.

How could this be? Last thing I remember was taking off in the airplane.

She teetered back to the hotel and leaned heavily on the front desk. There were two ladies sitting behind the counter wearing navy blue pant suits with gold name tags. "Could you please tell me if I'm registered at this hotel," she asked.

Rita looked up from her work, scowled at Carly, then got up from her chair and walked away. The second lady, Betty, looked at her and said, "Yes of course, Mrs. Davenport. I'll check our registry."

Carly may have been feeling groggy and lightheaded but she was sure the woman called her by name. "No, I don't see you on our records. I know for a fact that you are not registered here because you are not wearing the plastic bracelet we place on all our guests' wrists."

Carly looked down at her bare wrists in bewilderment. She'd never heard of that policy before but then again she hadn't been in a hotel in a lot of years. Money was tight and a holiday was a luxury they couldn't afford until now, apparently. "I'm sorry for troubling you," she said and turned to walk away.

"Wait," the lady said to her. "Have a seat in our lobby and I will check into something for you."

Carly was only too happy to sit down and rest. She needed to think and clear her head. She felt very strange. She watched the lady pick up the phone and turn away from Carly's sight. Suddenly the thought occurred to her that Betty was going to have her thrown out of the hotel. Not wanting that kind of embarrassment, Carly left the hotel and stepped into the warmth of the hot sun. The weather was tremendously different from the cold winter weather she left behind.

Carly wandered along the sidewalk looking around her. She tried to shade her eyes from the bright sun. The buildings did not look familiar. People were walking, cars were driving by, and they all seemed perfectly comfortable in their surroundings. Carly kept walking until she could walk no more. The heat was getting to her. She looked around for a bench to rest on and spied a police station.

She entered the noisy police station where a lot of people were in the waiting area. The frazzled officer at the desk was talking on the phone. Carly waited patiently for him to finish his conversation. He looked irritated with her and held up a finger indicating for Carly to wait a moment.

"What can I do for you, ma'am?"

Carly leaned in close to him and used a quiet voice to explain to him that she couldn't find her husband and that she didn't know where she was. The officer looked at her and said, "I'm really busy here, lady. This isn't a tea party. Why don't you call your husband on your cell phone?"

"I don't have a cell phone." Carly could hear snickers coming from the waiting area. She leaned in close to the officer and tried again, "I was on an airplane on my way to Las Vegas. My husband was flying the plane. I woke up in a strange hotel lobby with strangers all around me. I need to find my husband. Oh, please can you help me? Maybe the plane crashed and I have amnesia. My husband could be lying dead somewhere in a field with airplane pieces strewn all around him. Maybe if you check with the airport, they might know something."

The officer heaved a loud, heavy sigh. "Oh, all right. But this better be a legitimate problem or I'll be carting you off to the Institution."

Carly looked around the waiting room and decided to stay standing right where she was. The place was giving her the creeps. She watched the officer at the back of the room talking to another officer. Her officer shouted across the room to her, "The plane you mention is parked at the airport. There was no plane crash." *So much for privacy, Carly thought to herself.*

The two officers continued to talk to each other. They occasionally looked in Carly's direction and continued to talk. Carly quietly left the police station. She decided she better leave before she got arrested or carted off to the Institution. She would find a bench, sit down and regain her strength. Then she would come up with her next move.

"Mrs. Davenport," she heard her name being called. "I've been looking all over the place for you."

Carly turned to see Dave Hanson walking towards her. She was so relieved that she collapsed in a heap in his arms crying with joy to see a familiar face.

The police officer came charging down the street to find Carly. Seeing her with Dave, he stopped and watched.

"It's Okay, officer. I've come to take her back to Kenton. She wandered off but I have her now," Dave said with authority and winked at him. Better to let the police officer think he was taking Carly to Kenton. The fewer questions he had to answer the better. He hussled Carly away as quickly as he could before she could say anything to raise suspicions. He knew Sam would be furious with him when he found out that he had left Carly unattended.

The officer just nodded his head and watched them leave. He was more than familiar with Kenton Sanitarium. He wondered if his day could get any stranger. On the one hand it was good to have one less loony to worry about. On the other hand he wished this guy could hang around and take another one off his hands. Crazy Joe was due to arrive within the hour for his weekly measurement. The guy was convinced he was shrinking and that aliens were responsible. He heaved a heavy sigh and went back to the station. One of these days he hoped to win the lottery and get away from all of this craziness.

Chapter 6

Briefing Commander Steele

The HAHO door opened and Sam took a quick glance at his sleeping wife sprawled out on the divan before stepping out. The door was designed for him to parachute out of the belly of the plane, allowing him to jump safely clear of the jet's engines and avoid being sucked in to a spectacular death. Once again the Dave crew did a top-notch job of designing and executing their high tech upgrades.

It was good weather for jumping, blue sky as far as the eye could see, and Sam enjoyed himself. He loved the thrill of adventure. That was one of the reasons he was chosen to work on the undercover team. He gave everything he had to the missions, and he was proud of his high success rate. He watched the jet fly off into the distance and hoped Carly would be safe.

The recovery team of 3 was waiting in the speed boat. They plucked Sam out of the Pacific Ocean and whisked him away to rendezvous with the waiting submarine. From there Sam's destination was to a top secret remote location in the Arctic.

Tuktoyaktuk, NWT, or Tuk, on the shores of the Arctic Ocean at the uppermost edge of Canada, is a land of dogsleds, Midnight Sun, Northern Lights and pingos. Pingos are mounds of earth-covered ice that can reach up to 70 meters. They are non-glacial landforms formed by ground ice which develops during winter months as the temperature falls.

Present weather forecast was -19 degrees Celsius. The wind was blowing from the southwest. There were a few clouds with a visibility of 24.1 kilometers. 5 cm of snow was expected to add to the already white terrain.

This wasn't a fixed military location, just a temporary base. Whenever there was activity going on in Russia, they liked to be nearby and ready. The Commander's aide escorted Sam to the log cabin being used as temporary quarters.

He saluted Commander Steele and his salute was returned. Sam was dressed in his Arctic gear as required for the cold environment. DEU's as they are called. Distinct Environment Uniform. At 5' 7" tall, Sam was a little chubby, but it wasn't noticeable under all the layers of clothing he was wearing. His blonde hair was freshly cut for this visit with a high officer as per military regulations.

The two men entered the Commander's private quarters and the aide left them alone. Commander Steele went to the stone fireplace, removed the screen cover, and poked at the crackling logs. Sam removed his white camouflage winter parka and hung it on the coat rack. White boots were left by the door. The warmth of the log cabin was a welcome relief. A luxury that only the Commander was privileged to have. The Commander replaced the screen and the two men sat in comfortable gray leather wing chairs in front of the roaring fire. Grant was proud of his floor to ceiling stone fireplace.

"Welcome to my humble dwellings in the Great White North. We're all lucky we came in November before the real cold hits this place. How is that wife of yours? Did you bring pictures of your new grandson?"

"Thank you, sir. The baby is well. He gets bigger every time I see him. Chubby little cheeks and he's starting to smile. Carly, on the other hand, is in danger but she doesn't know about it. I couldn't blow my cover with her, and I couldn't leave her at home by herself. I left her in the hands of the Dave crew. It was all so sudden and we didn't anticipate this. Archie sent the package to my house; Carly accepted it and signed for it. They now know where my wife is and I expect they will make an attempt to get to me through my family."

"Yes, I understand the seriousness of the situation. Family means everything to us and we look out for each other," Grant Steele nodded his head. "The Dave crew is in charge of her? I don't like the sound of that. We better make alternate arrangements or she'll never forgive you. They may be gifted at designing and creating military tools but escorting a sophisticated lady around is not one of their talents."

"Yes, thank you, sir."

"Drop the sir stuff while we're in private, Sam. You and I go back a long way. Golly gosh, our wives are sisters after all! I'll get on the horn as soon as we're done here and get an army of agents assigned to take care of Carly for you. The Dave crew is well meaning and they would give it their best, but our Carly requires special treatment. If all goes well, she won't even know she is being taken care of by highly trained secret agent bodyguards. I think you'll need to treat your wife to a romantic vacation when this mission is completed, though, to make it up to her."

"I think you're right about that!"

"What about the rest of your family? The kids and grandkids won't be safe for too long either. Once they discover Carly's not home they could go looking for your kids."

"I left Ethan in charge of them. He's very capable and has lots of friends he can enlist. He's aware of the danger. He's smart enough not to ask questions and he assured me he won't let anything happen to them."

"Good man, that Ethan. I quite agree with you. He'll do a bang-up job on his end. Any chance we can sign him up for our family undercover team? Still, I'll assign a couple of agents to keep an eye on all of your family, just to be on the safe side. I wonder if they'd agree to go on a vacation?"

Grant Steele got up to make coffee. Sam followed him into the kitchen. "Check inside the pantry and see if there are any cookies in there. One good thing about being in a remote military base is they stock us up with great cookies. A staple at all meetings, you know! I love the peanut butter ones if you can find some like that." They chatted and laughed over old family stories before taking their coffee with them to sit by the fire again.

"What updates did you bring of the mission?"

"Agent Archie is believed to be dead, sir. He sent details of a terrorist scheme to steal an abandoned nuclear submarine from the Soviet Submarine Graveyard." Sam passed the photos to Grant. "The group is working under the guise of scrap collectors. Those photos show them repairing and upgrading the submarine to working order. The particular submarine they have is loaded with 7 aging nuclear warheads. It wouldn't take much for them to spruce the thing up and add a robotic mechanism and then use it as a weapon of mass destruction. We have reason to believe they intend to obliterate a large civilian population. Much like marching around the walls of the city seven times before the walls came tumbling down."

"I'll get my men on this immediately," Grant assured Sam. "Do we know the name of the terrorist group?"

"No, not yet, sir. My team is working on that. We think we recognized two of our own agents in a few photos. This is very unexpected and puts us all on high alert. We can trust no one until we get to the bottom of this. As soon as we find anything out we'll let you know."

Chapter 7

Bubble Bath

"Betty phoned me and told me you left the hotel," Dave explained. "She was worried you'd get lost. I told her to keep an eye on you while I went to run an errand. I was only gone five minutes. Man you were out like a light!" Dave held the restaurant door open for Carly to enter.

"Where is Sam?"

"Oh well, we had some engine problems and had to land the plane here on Summerview Island. We didn't make it to Vegas. Now we have to work on repairs before we can leave here," Dave told her. He thought he was doing pretty good with the story he'd memorized.

"Will you answer my question? Where is Sam? He wouldn't just disappear and leave me alone in some strange place without a decent explanation." Carly was not amused and wanted an answer.

The waitress appeared and asked, "How many in your party?"

"Two," Dave looked at her, "Are you hungry? This place has great food. You'll feel much better if you eat something."

Carly was feeling steamed that Dave was avoiding her question. Something smelled good and she did feel hungry. Once they were seated in a booth she leaned forward and hissed her question at Dave again.

"Where is Sam? Has something happened to him?"

"Well, that's the thing. You remember Archie, don't you? Well, unfortunately we got word that he died suddenly. Sam had to go to his family immediately seeing as how he's the guy in charge of the estate and all."

"Oh no, I remember Archie. What happened?"

"Well I'm not exactly sure, I think his heart stopped or something."
Dave chided himself for that answer because nobody really knew
the specifics of how old Archie died, but he was sure his heart
stopped at some point. The sad realities of life in the spy business.

"Archie was a good man," Carly sighed. "He came to our place for
dinners many times. Sam got along good with him."

"Yeah, so anyways, Sam said I should give this to you." He pulled
a shiny new credit card out of his wallet and handed it to Carly.
"He said you could go shopping and get yourself something nice to
wear. He wanted to make up for not being here. He said he'll
come back as soon as he can."

"Oh," Carly was startled to see a credit card. She wondered where
the heck Sam was getting all this money all of a sudden. Still, she
would like to change her clothes, and the thought of shopping did
cheer her up. She felt like she'd been wearing her jeans for days.
She looked at Dave suspiciously, and then took the credit card.

They ate hamburgers and fries for their lunch. Carly didn't feel so
good after eating and excused herself to go to the ladies room. She
got there just in time to hurl her lunch into the toilet. She cleaned
herself up and returned to the table gingerly to ask Dave if he
could take her to the hotel to rest.

"I don't understand why I feel so ill," she whined to Dave.

"You're likely suffering jet lag. Let's get you to the store to get a
change of clothes. You can rest in the car on our way out of town.
There's this place I have to go to get some parts to fix the plane.
You can have a rest there."

Carly didn't like that idea too much but went along with it. She
intended to grab the first thing she saw so they could get on their
way quickly. The promise to get to rest was forefront on her mind.

****

Dave eased the car into the garage and parked. Carly was passed out in the passenger seat. He had slipped a sleeping pill into her coke at lunch and waited patiently until it took effect. He was a little worried she upchucked it into the toilet after lunch so he encouraged her to have a cup of tea to settle her stomach before they left to go shopping. He slipped a second pill into her tea when she wasn't looking. She was so groggy by the time they got to the mall that Dave enlisted the help of the hot blonde clerk named Tammy to choose some things for Carly.

Agent Campbell helped Dave get Carly inside the house. Campbell carried her to the guest room and placed her gently on the four poster bed. Agent Monique placed the shopping bags on the floor and sat down in the chair beside Carly.

"I'll stay here until she wakes up," Monique told the two men. "You go ahead and make arrangements. I'll be along once she is ready for dinner. We'll be eating late. She's really out of it."

****

Carly woke to the sound of a bathtub being filled. She looked around the massive strange room in bewilderment. She was lying in the most beautiful four poster bed she had ever seen. The dark cherry wood was gorgeous. A puffy white duvet covered her and the white pillows felt soft and wonderful. She was content to stay in the luxurious bed for a long time. If only Sam were here to enjoy it with her.

"Ah, you're awake," Monique said in a cheery voice. "I thought you were going to sleep for hours. I ran a bath for you if you are interested. It will freshen you up before dinner. I'm Monique, by the way. You are a guest in my home. Once you get freshened up and dressed, we can get to know each other better at dinner. We love to entertain and you are a captive audience that we can't resist."

"Oh, hi," Carly managed a groggy reply. "I must have fallen asleep in the car. Is Dave here too?"

"Yes, he is negotiating the purchase of parts for his plane. My husband loves to see airplanes restored to their original beauty. He and Dave will be at it for hours. We'll interrupt them for dinner, though." She smiled as she followed Carly to the tub. "I hung your clothes in the closet for you. You'll find everything you need to dress for dinner. You certainly did a lot of shopping before you got here. We like to dress up for dinner and you have purchased some very appropriate items. Give me a shout when you are ready and I will take you to the dining room."

"OK, thank you." She wondered how difficult it could be to find a dining room?

Carly undressed and dropped her clothes on the floor. Her bladder was full so she took care of that business. Then she climbed into the wonderfully warm bubble bath. It was a corner whirlpool bathtub with massaging jets next to a large window frosted for privacy. She could lean back and stretch her legs out without her toes touching the end of the tub. She thought she had died and gone to heaven. She lounged in the lavender scented bath until her fingers looked like prunes. She moved to the shower stall adjacent to the tub and washed her hair. The shampoo smelled like almonds. It felt good to be clean again.

The clothes were hanging in the closet just as Monique said they were. She was so tired at the department store that she let Dave pick out her purchases. She didn't pay too much attention to what he threw on the counter. She told him her size and he went to it. The clerk must have helped him because there were some pretty sexy undies in the bag.

She put on the white lace bra and matching panties and looked at herself in the full length mirror. *"Not bad for an old gal,"* she said to herself. She blow dried her hair and then put on her make-up. Thank goodness she had her own make-up in her tote bag; she couldn't imagine what Dave and the sexy sales clerk would have picked out for her.

Next she put on the red dress. She was surprised at Dave's taste in clothing. It was actually a cute little dress. It had spaghetti straps and it hung loosely just above her knees. A little sexier than what she would normally wear. She inspected herself in the mirror. It was a nice shade of red and accented her long curly brown hair. She thought her arms and legs looked too flabby, not to mention her butt.

Inside the bag she found a pair of red stiletto shoes. *"Who the heck thought I would wear shoes like these?"* she wondered. *"I haven't worn heels in a very long time."*

There were red hair combs in the bag as well as a variety of barrettes. She selected a set of red barrettes to wear and left her hair loose to fall down her back. She giggled when she saw the tiny little red earrings. Whoever did the shopping didn't think she needed splashy earrings.

When she opened the door, Monique was waiting for her. They descended the stairs but Carly was having trouble with her heels. Her feet wobbled something terrible. She stopped to look out the wall of glass windows along the spiral staircase. The sun was setting, the clouds were a soft shade of pink, and the view of the blue ocean was lovely.

"Let's take the elevator the rest of the way down," Monique suggested. "I'm sure you won't appreciate walking down the remaining two flights of stairs."

After dinner, Monique gave the guests a tour of the pool. It was an infinity pool. When they stood in the pool house and looked out, it looked as though the pool dropped off the edge of the cliff. The view, again, was superb. You could see the ocean and the mountains in the distance. Carly wondered what the view would look like in the daylight. Carly wished Sam could have bought a house with a pool like this one instead of a silly airplane.

Dave announced that it was time for Carly to leave. He had a taxi waiting to take her to the airport. Carly was relieved to hear that. She would much prefer to return home. She said good bye to her hosts and thanked them for their hospitality, then followed Dave to the waiting car. Dave went around to talk to the driver, and then he returned to help Carly get in the back seat.

"I will follow behind you. I've got a lot of parts for the plane to bring with me. It'll be easier if you ride in the cab."

He closed the cab door before Carly could protest and the cab sped off.

Chapter 8

Middle of Nowhere

It was raining and the taxi driver had the windshield wipers on full speed. He pulled the car over to the side of the road and stopped.

"OK, you get out now," he turned around and said to Carly.

"What do you mean?" Carly asked incredulously. "You are supposed to take me to the airport. This is the middle of nowhere! I'm not getting out here!"

"No, the man said you get out here."

Carly looked out the window into the dark world. She didn't want to get out here. The cab driver pulled a gun out and pointed it at her. She got out pretty quick. The cab spun his tires and flung mud all over Carly as he left.

She stood on the shoulder of the road and looked around. It was very dark and there was nothing but wilderness as far as the eye could see. She was wet from the pouring rain and she was cold. When she got her hands on Dave, he was going to get a piece of her mind! She was not amused to say the least. Friday morning she got on an airplane with hopes of having a relaxing holiday, she woke up in a strange hotel lobby where she embarrassed herself with her snoring and drooling; she wandered around a strange town like she was homeless and now she was standing on a deserted highway getting rained on with no idea where she should go next. She didn't even know what day it was anymore!

Remembering that Dave said he would follow behind the cab, she looked down the deserted road in hopes he would show up soon to rescue her. There was no traffic in sight. Walking on the road was not so great when one was wearing stiletto heels. Carly managed to walk in them half decently at the house but her feet were now sore. What she would give for a comfortable pair of sneakers right about now. She wished she could close her eyes and magically put herself back into that lovely and warm bubble bath.

After a few steps she decided she should probably get to the side of the road in case a car came zipping by and knocked her down. One step to the right and her heel sunk into the mud. She tried to pull her foot out of the mud and almost succeeded until her other leg lost balance and she fell down. At this point she decided to take off the stilettos and walk in bare feet. How bad could it be? She was already covered in mud. She took off the shoes and flung them as far away as she could. Of course, the second shoe didn't leave her hand on time and she ended up clunking it onto her head. No worries, she thought helplessly, the pouring rain will wash the mud out of my hair in no time.

Sitting in the mud, she decided to allow herself a good cry. She sobbed and sobbed. Nobody could hear her, she felt ridiculous, and she missed her husband. Nobody had ever pointed a gun at her before. Who points guns at unsuspecting cab passengers? She yelled out to nobody in particular, "I'm all alone in the wilderness, if there are any starving animals out there now would be a good time to come and get me." Well she didn't really mean for any hungry animals to eat her. It just felt better to shout it out. She could barely hear her own voice over the sound of the pouring rain.

A sound caught Carly's attention. She didn't know if it was her imagination or if she really could hear something moving out there. Maybe it wasn't a good idea to yell. She stood up on her wobbly legs and started walking. It was then that a light came on in the distance. Hallelujah, she could see a house. It was so wonderful to see a house. She would walk to that house and ask to use their phone. She would phone someone to come and get her and then she would go home to her safe and comfy house. Finally!

By the time she climbed the steps to the porch of the house she was wet and filthy and feeling mighty miserable. Her cut and aching feet sported a few blisters. She had her hand in the air ready to knock when the door opened up. An old woman with short white hair stood before her. She was tiny enough and looked to be in her eighties.

"Well it's about time you got here. Me and Walter was about to give up on you and go to bed."

Carly was gob smacked. "You were expecting me?"

"Of course we was," she said. "That nice young man come and dropped off a bag of clothes for you about an hour ago. The dang cab driver was told to drop you off at our front door. I'll give him a talking to if I ever see him again! Well don't just stand there, git yerself in here. Them coyotes are nasty this time of night. They'd eat you alive if they knew you was here."

Carly's eyes went big and wide remembering how she was shouting at the wilderness not too long ago. The thought of coyotes out there made her feel grateful to find shelter. She scooted inside where she felt safer. She could see an old man in the other room sitting in a chair in front of the TV. The tiny TV had a blank white screen. Carly got the impression the station had shut down for the night.

"Walter, you about ready? It's time to get you to bed."

"Awww, I ain't tired, Ruthie! My show's about to come on. I don't wanner miss it."

"I'm Ruthie," the old lady had to look way up to speak to Carly. "That there's Walter. Don't mind him, he just likes to watch his shows. You'll be staying in the den. We keep a bed in there in case we gets company. I put fresh sheets on it about a month ago. We ain't had no guests in at least a week. We're perty much by ourselves out here. You want me to fix up something to eat? Walter, you shut that TV down. I'll be in to git you ready in a minute."

"Gall darn woman, I told you I ain't tired."

"You can sleep in as long as you want in the morning," she explained. "Your driver will be here to git you at 7:00 am sharp. I put yer bag in the room there for ya. Don't mind us in the mornin. We get up early so's Walter can watch his shows. We'll try an be quiet fer ya ta git yer rest. You go on in and rest up, I'll make you a cup of tea and some toast. I'll call fer ya when it's ready."

Carly went into the spare room and closed the door. She sat on the bed. It was a foldaway cot but anything looked good right about now as long as it was dry and warm. She could hear Ruthie and Walter walking to their room. Walter didn't sound like he moved too well; she could hear feet shuffling along the floor. "I gotta sit on the pot, Ruthie."

"All right, but don't you fall asleep on the pot. You know what happened last time, you banged yer head on the towel bar and got blood everywhere. I ain't too good at hammerin nails into the wall to fix it right. Don't make me have ta fix it agin."

"OK Ruthie, I'll be careful where I fall."

Ruthie poked her head into the room to talk to Carly. "If'n you need to use the john you can have a shower and stuff tonight. You look a mess. I just gotter git Walter off the pot first. He cain't reach his arms back to wipe his butt so I gotta do it fer him. You won't disturb us once we get in bed and Walter takes his hearing aids out."

"OK, thanks for letting me know," Carly answered back.

Looking inside the bag that was dropped off for her, she saw a clean set of clothes. There was a track suit, sneakers, socks, underwear, and a blonde wig. "What on earth did she need a wig for?" She left the wig in the bag.

Ruthie and Walter finished shuffling to their room and closed the door. Carly took the opportunity to have a quick shower. The water was lukewarm but she didn't care. She just needed to wash all that mud off. Then she put on the clean underwear and track suit. She found the tea and toast that Ruthie left out for her and sat at the kitchen table to enjoy it. Then she climbed into bed. As she stretched out to get comfortable one of the bed legs broke and she found herself lying with her head down and her feet up in the air. She was too tired to care. All she wanted to do was sleep. At least she was in a bed with warm covers and there would be a driver here in the morning to take her to the airport.

The sound of gun shots startled Carly awake. She jumped out of bed and opened the bedroom door to see what was going on. There was Ruthie holding a rifle and closing the front door. "Did I wake you? Don't you worry none, I had this ol six shooter since I was a wee thing. My ol pappy taught me how to shoot. I never miss when I sets my mind to it. Them coyotes was scratching at the door trying to get in the house. I shot one of em and the others got away. You go on back to sleep now. Ruthie will take good care of ya."

Ruthie waddled down the hall and Carly watched her in stunned silence. She went back to bed and shivered at the thought of the strange events she had been through in the last couple of days. She said a silent prayer thanking God for keeping those coyotes away from her.

Chapter 9

Another Cab Ride

The sound of Ruthie and Walter shuffling around and chattering woke Carly. She snuggled under the covers and tried to go back to sleep.

"Time to get up now!" Ruthie hollered. "Your cab is here. I told ya he'd be here at 7:00 am sharp. I'll keep him occupied while you get ready. Come on outside when you're up and at it."

Carly groaned. She still felt very tired but was energized at the thought of going home. Everything would be much better when she could collapse into her own comfy bed. She dragged herself to the washroom to brush her teeth and then went out to the waiting taxi cab.

"You come back anytime now," Ruthie said as she closed the cab door and waved goodbye.

Carly hadn't seen the yard in the daylight. She was amazed to see several cameras set up along the driveway to the highway. There was barbed wire along the fence too. Ruthie and Walter were one strange couple. What on earth would they need cameras for? They lived out in the middle of nowhere. Carly searched but didn't see any dead coyotes. Ruthie said she shot one in the night but there was no evidence of it anywhere.

"How long will it take us to get to the airport?"

"It'll take about an hour, miss."

"OK, thank you."

Carly rested her head on the door and slept. She was very tired lately and didn't understand why. She intended to see her doctor when she got home and have a complete physical check up.

A loud crunching noise woke Carly with a start. A big black car had side swiped the cab and they were forced off the road. The cab came to a stop and Carly heard a gunshot. The cab driver slumped forward and then fell down sideways into the front seat. With her heart racing, Carly tried desperately to open her door and get out.

A very big man in a black suit with black hair wearing dark sunglasses grabbed her arm when she got out of the cab. "Hello Mrs. Davenport," he said in a thick Russian accent. "Nice to meet you. I have friends who want to give you leetle tea party. Your husband is naughty boy. He spoil Dmitri's fun. Dmitri no like that. Dmitri like to have fun. We convince your husband to see things my way soon enough. He will come for you and we will keel him."

Carly whimpered at the sight of him and wondered if he was going to shoot her too. More guns. Why was this happening to her? She hugged her tote bag close to her body and then had an idea. She swung her bag at the man and ran for it as fast as her legs could take her. He grabbed her bag and flung it, spilling the contents all over the place. Then he caught up to her and knocked her to the ground. He stepped on her back with his foot and held her in place. He tied her hands behind her back with rope. Then he put duct tape across her mouth, picked her up with one hand and avoided her kicking legs. He placed her unceremoniously into the trunk of his car and slammed the lid shut. "You get first class ride in Dmitri's car. You weel like place we go to even better."

Screaming didn't really work with the duct tape on her mouth. It hurt when she moved her mouth and it tore her skin. She had tasted blood when he knocked her down and she was certain she had a fat lip. Her right cheek burned and felt like it had little rocks stuck in her skin. Her knees hurt too from landing on them first before smashing her head into the ground. Squirming didn't do much good in the tight space and it only added to the pain she was experiencing. Crying allowed her to feel sorry for herself but wouldn't help her escape. If she still had those stiletto shoes she could have kicked that man good. She read an article once about what to do if you got kidnapped and locked in the trunk of a car. They said you should try to kick out the tail lights and get the attention of the car behind you. It was very dark inside the trunk and Carly didn't know for sure if she had the strength but she would try anything. She lifted her legs to kick when she was tossed to the back of the trunk by a sudden acceleration of the car.

Tires were squealing and the car was weaving back and forth. The car came to a sudden stop and Carly was tossed in the other direction like a sack of potatoes. She could hear gunshots and decided now was a good time to cry again. She said a silent prayer in expectation that she was about to die. The ropes around her wrists prevented her from crossing herself but she imagined thinking about it would work just as well. She could hear someone near the car and held her breath as she heard the trunk being fiddled with.

"Hey there," Ruthie said to her as she opened the trunk. "Looks like you met Dmitri. We took care of him for you. Roll around there so I can take the ropes off you."

The first thing Carly wanted to do with her freed hands was take the duct tape off her mouth.

"Best do that real quick like you would remove a bandage," Ruthie told her. "It's gonna sting judging by the damage you already done to yer face."

Walter was sitting in the car watching them. Ruthie helped Carly out of the trunk and walked her over to her car. Carly wasn't surprised by anything anymore. Ruthie drove a shiny new black Charger.

"I can't leave without my bag." Carly ran to get her bag, trying not to look at the dead Dmitri leaning against the steering wheel of his car. His head was turned in her direction but his eyes were looking down in an eerie way. The blood spatter covered the car window.

She wandered all over hecks half acre picking up her belongings and putting them back into her bag. "A man should never come between a woman and her purse," she muttered. "Tea party indeed!"

Ruthie had a lead foot as she sped away from the gruesome scene. Carly watched the speedometer rising quickly yet the ride felt incredibly smooth. "We got friends'll come and take care of that mess back there. Don't you worry none."

"What was that all about?" Carly couldn't control the sobs. The emotions were taking over. Things were getting so out of control. "I had a cab driver point a gun at me and get out into the darkest and wettest middle of nowhere I ever saw, then a second cab driver got shot and killed in front of me. Who goes around kidnapping innocent women? Why did that horrible man say my husband spoiled his fun?"

"You just set back there and relax. I'll explain everything when we get home. Ruthie's gonna take good care of you from now on."

"Home? I want to get to the airport and go to MY home."

"There's been a change of plans. Dmitri's only one problem taken care of. He has plenty more friends looking to kidnap you, and they are all deadly killers."

"Don't you go telling her we's spies, Ruthie," said Walter.

"Oh you hush up, Walter. I'll tell her everything when we get back to the house. I could sure use a cup of tea right about now."

"Can we have some of that macaroni in a box that I like? I'm hungry. I like ketchup with it too. Don't forget the ketchup. I'm gonna eat mine in front of the TV. My show's will be on and I cain't miss 'em. Do we have any of that ice cream left over? Cookies too, I like the little animal cracker ones."

Somehow Carly decided she was relieved to be going back to Ruthie and Walter's house. Life had gotten awfully strange lately and she'd much prefer to hang out with these quirky folks as opposed to that Dmitri and his deadly *keeler* friends. Ruthie seemed to be pretty capable with a gun and Carly could use that kind of friend right about now.

The thought of macaroni and ketchup made Carly feel homesick. That was what her four-year-old grandson, Curtis, liked to eat. She wished he were here to give her a big hug and tell her everything was going to be all right.

Chapter 10

More Near Truths

Back at the house, Walter went straight to his chair in front of the TV. He started flipping through the channels until he settled on a game show. The laugh track could be heard loud and clear, but he turned it up even more.

Ruthie busied herself in the kitchen putting on the tea kettle and rummaging through the cupboards. "Do you like macaroni? I can fix you up something else if you like. I'm a pretty good cook."

"No, I couldn't eat anything right now," Carly answered. "My stomach has been acting up and I'm pretty stressed out."

"OK, toast it is. Walter would like some toast with his macaroni too."

"Don't forget the ketchup," he yelled from the living room.

"I'd really like you to tell me what's going on," Carly said to her. "I can't take any more of this strangeness. Should we call the police?"

"No, no. We got people that'll let the police know what they need to know. This here is top secret spy business. I got my instructions to watch over you after you left in the cab this morning. Too bad I didn't get the message before you left."

Carly accepted the china tea cup from Ruthie. Her hands shook and the cup and saucer rattled until she managed to put it down on the table. Ruthie left the room quietly and came back with an electric blanket, which she plugged into the wall next to the kitchen table. She wrapped it around Carly and turned on the control. "This'll warm you up once it kicks in. It'll make you feel better."

"Thank you," Carly said trying to stop her lips from shivering. "Can you tell me why that Dmitri man said my husband was a naughty boy? He wanted to kill him, and how did he know my name, and how did you know about all of this to come and rescue me?"

"I'm gonna bake some brownies while I'm in the kitchen. We haven't had them in quite a while. Do you like brownies? They're one of my specialties." Ruthie was stalling while she thought up a good story to tell Carly.

"No brownies for me, I'm afraid." Carly made a dash for the washroom where the sound of her vomiting filled the little house. She returned to the kitchen fifteen minutes later. On the table, Ruthie had placed two little white pills beside a fresh cup of tea.

"Take those pills. It's something gentle to settle your tummy and help you rest. You've been through enough for now. Don't give me any lip now. You go on and get yourself tucked in bed and have a sleep. You'll feel better when you wake up. We can talk then."

Carly didn't argue. She felt terribly weak and welcomed the chance to crawl in a safe warm bed and sleep.

****

The sound of Walter snoring in front of the TV woke Carly several hours later. She found Ruthie in the kitchen preparing dinner.

"Well, howdy, stranger. You missed out on my famous macaroni for lunch. Never fear I'm making pork chops for supper. You had a good long sleep. Feeling better now?"

"Yes, Ruthie. I needed that rest. I hope my stomach will stay settled."

"I have more of those pills if you need some. You just let me know." Ruthie patted Carly on the shoulder and pointed to a kitchen chair. "Now, let's sit down while supper's in the oven and Walter's sleeping." She pulled her chair close to Carly's until their knees were touching. "That Dmitri was a very bad man. Always been up to no good." Ruthie waved her finger in the air. "He got mad when your Sam walked into the middle of a bank robbery. Your Sam's a brave man." She stopped and smiled. "He stopped those robbers single handed." She nodded her head. "That's why Dmitri came for you. He knew Sam wouldn't let anything happen to you." She patted Carly's knee. "Don't you worry none, cuz your Sam's under police protection now. They got him hiding real good and safe until they can bring them bank robbers to court." Ruthie leaned toward the table and swept a few crumbs off the placemat. "Once they's behind bars for a good long time, Sam will be able to come home to you. Meanwhile, you can stay here with us." She went to the sink to get a wet dishcloth and returned to wipe the table clean. "Nobody messes with me and Walter. We might look old and feeble but we are none to be messed with." Sitting down again, she gave Carly a motherly look, "Dmitri's got other friends out there and we're ready for 'em."

"But how do you know all this?" Carly asked.

"We are what you call secret agents. Sam told the cops where you were and they got in touch with me. We got strict orders to keep you safe and sound until this whole thing's over."

"What about my family? My kids and grandkids. I would like to talk to them and let them know I'm going to be away from home for a while."

"Nope, you cain't do that nohow. Everything has to be kept real secret like until the judge sends them bad guys to jail. Your whole family's under police protection."

"How long will that be?"

"Oh it could take up to six months." Ruthie lied. She didn't really know how long Carly would be staying with them but she didn't want Carly getting her hopes up too early. The mission Sam was really working on would take some time to work through. "Them police protection folks said you should go out shopping with that shiny new credit card they gave you. Shopping is the best therapy for you right now. I'll get my son, Brett, to take you. Ain't nobody gonna mess with you while he's looking out fer ya. He'll be your bodyguard."

The idea of shopping didn't really hit the spot for Carly at that moment but she thought she could pick up a few necessities for now. So the police protection agency provided that credit card. Carly had a few ideas suddenly pop into her mind like a ray of sunshine. Maybe she could manage a shopping spree after all.

Chapter 11

Agent Monique and Agent Campbell

Monique paced back and forth in the glass-enclosed balcony overlooking the driveway. She ran the fingers of her left hand through her short strawberry blonde hair and held the phone to her ear with the right. Listening intently, she finally spoke, "Who do they think they are? Dmitri was my best man! I'll make them pay for this, you mark my words. Where's that little bitch now? I'll get her myself. Sam won't be so cocky when he sees we have his little wifey. We'll get him to see things our way!" She tossed the phone down on the table and stormed into the house. "Campbell!" she hollered. "Campbell, come here quick. They've messed up our plans."

When there was no response from Campbell, she stormed through the massive house toward the infinity pool. Campbell was swimming laps and stopped when he saw her arrive. "Hey, what's up?"

"Dmitri's been killed. The Davenport woman got away. Those people are giving me a headache."

Campbell climbed out of the pool and grabbed a towel from the lounge chair and rubbed his black hair. Water was dripping down his sculpted body. "Take it easy, sweets. We can still do this. We just have to be calm and think it through. They're all a bunch of simpletons. They think we are on their side. We'll just think of a way to get Mrs. Davenport to stay with us here. Then she'll be putty in our hands. It's all too simple, love. Sam won't let any harm come to her. Now cheer up and take a dip in the pool with me." He pulled her into a hug and walked her over to the edge of the pool where they fell into the water together.

"You take such good care of me," she said to him, shaking her soaking wet hair but deep in thought. "What would I do without you?" Monique seemed oblivious that she was in the pool fully dressed. "I like your plan. I think it could work. It sounds so deliciously simple." She smiled and they shared a passionate kiss. "As long as we get to use the submarine. I'm so excited to see it blow up. All those explosions...yummy. It makes me all goose bumpy just thinking about it."

"Yes, darling. I'm sure you'll get to see the submarine blow. Now stop worrying. Your forehead is getting all crinkled. Just think nice thoughts, like how wonderful you'll look when you wear all those jewels. We'll be even more rich and sexy than we already are!"

"Oh you say the nicest things to cheer me up."

"How about you take those wet clothes off and we'll pretend you're a helpless mermaid and I'm a pirate."

"Why do I have to be the helpless one? I'd rather pretend to be the killer mermaid that's going to take you captive as my sex slave."

"You make me all tingly. I love my little dominatrix." They splashed about giggling and disappeared under the water. Monique's clothes floated to the top one piece at a time.

****

First thing the next morning, Brett arrived to take Carly shopping as promised. Brett was a strong and sturdy man. His brown hair was in a tidy crew cut. He wore a black suit, white shirt, green tie, and black shoes. Carly looked him over suspiciously when he walked into the house.

"This is my son, Brett," Ruthie introduced him. "He's going to take you shopping."

"I'll get my tote bag and I'm ready to go. Don't leave without me, Brett."

Brett stepped just inside the door. He did not speak to anyone. He looked down at Ruthie and nodded.

"OK, I'm ready. Let's go. This shouldn't take too long. Do you need me to bring anything back?"

"Nope, oh no, I got everything here I need."

"Can you bring back some of those crackers in them whacky shapes?" Walter hollered from the living room. "And some cheese too."

"Now Walter, you know cheese makes you fart. I ain't sleepin' with you if you're gonna be farting all night long. It stinks like heck."

"Aww Ruthie, I ain't had no crackers an' cheese in ages. I want some. Please, lemmie show ya I can be good. I won't let no farts go all night. I promise."

Carly chuckled to herself as she ran out of the house to the waiting car. It was a black one, just like the car Dmitri drove. She wondered why everyone was so fond of black cars in this place. This time she planned to sit in the front seat in comfort. No more trunks for her.

She looked at Brett as he held the door open for her, "no offense but you don't look anything like Ruthie and Walter." They are both so short and slim."

"I was adopted," Brett replied with no emotion. He closed Carly's door and went around to the driver's side. Once he had the engine running he said, "Ruthie, er, I mean mom makes great brownies. I could never resist them. You tried them yet?"

"Not yet. She made a batch last night but I wasn't feeling too well. Maybe later when I get back I'll try a sample. You always dress up like that to go shopping?"

"Yes."

"Do you have any other suits? I mean, that aren't black?"

"No."

"Do you have many ties?"

"No."

"You are a man of few words."

Brett followed Carly around store to store without saying a word. She bought herself some clothes and necessary items. Once she took care of her own immediate needs, she skipped along to the next stores with an evil grin on her face. She would simply explain that she required a great deal of shopping therapy to get over the horrible trunk ordeal.

****

"We're back!" Carly shouted as she walked in the house. "Brett's just helping me bring in a few things."

Ruthie stood in the kitchen with her mouth open and just stared. The groceries were everywhere on the table, on the floor, and on the counter. "What in tar nations is this all about?"

"Well, I figured if the police protection people were going to be so kind as to give me a credit card, I would put it to good use."

"I ain't got no room for all that frozen stuff you got there."

"Oh not to worry, Ruthie. The freezer will be delivered here tomorrow. Just squeeze all you can into the fridge for now. Anything that doesn't fit in the fridge, we'll start baking. I bought lots of freezer containers. I love baking. We'll have fun. We can start with a huge batch of chili."

"Did you get me that cheese and crackers I asked fer?"

"Yes, Walter. I got lots of cheese and all kinds of crackers. Fruit too, I like to eat apple slices with cheese and grapes too."

"What kinda cheese did ya git?"

"Cheddar, gouda, mozzarella, marble. All kinds."

"Jes as long as I don't fart up a storm on Ruthie. I like grapes."

Carly went into the living room and sat on the couch next to Walter's chair. "I ordered you a new TV. It'll be here tomorrow too. You're going to love it."

"A new TV fer me? Hoooweeeee. Did ya hear that Ruthie? A new TV fer me."

"I ordered a new bed for the spare room too. The one in there now has a broken leg. After I'm gone you can entertain your guests in style."

"Well what'd ya git fer me?" Ruthie asked.

"For you, Ruthie, I got you a nice comfy chair so you can sit next to Walter and watch the shows on the new TV together."

"I ain't had a new chair in ages. I'm gonna like that chair a whole lot, Carly. Thank you."

"Is that handsome son of yours going to stay for supper? How about it, Brett? I think there are brownies for dessert unless Walter and Ruthie ate them all on us."

"Aww shucks no, we ain't had none of them brownies yet. An Ruthie made us a pot roast fer supper. An those little roasted potaters. Cain't ya smell it cookin? I'm so hungry I could eat a horse."

"Well, how about it, Brett? Are you staying?"

"Yes ma'am."

"Then we better get these groceries put away."

"Hot dang, Walter. We ain't had no company for dinner in a long time. I'm a likin this."

"Just wait 'til you see all the new ties I bought for Brett," Carly said as she hunted through her shopping bags. "If I'm to have a bodyguard, I want him to have a little style." She held up several ties for everyone to see. "Oh, and I ordered a comfy set of patio furniture for your front porch. They have thick floral cushions. It'll be nice for us to take in the evening air together."

Chapter 12

Domestic Invasion

Carly woke up bright and early with every intention of cooking up a storm. If she was going to stay in this house for a couple of months, she might as well make the best of it. These people could use some home cooking and Carly had lots of time on her hands to do it. She would show her appreciation to Ruthie and Walter for letting her stay in their home.

Dressed in new cream color Capri pants and brown t-shirt she headed to the kitchen to get started. She pulled the new slow cooker out of the box and washed it. Then she rummaged through the fridge for all the ingredients to make chili as promised. As she piled the vegetables for chopping, she noticed a movement on the front porch. She froze with fear and stopped breathing. She grabbed the knife she was going to use to chop the vegetables and took a deep breath.

Peeking out the screen door, she saw Brett sleeping in a kitchen chair and looking mighty uncomfortable. "Good morning, sunshine!" she said brightly when she realized it was a false alarm.

Brett woke up and stood facing her. "Is everything all right?"

"Yes, everything is fine. I thought you were a prowler. What the heck are you doing sleeping outside on the porch? Wouldn't the couch be more comfortable?"

"Just keeping an eye out. Wouldn't want any intruders to hurt my family."

"You always sleep in a chair on the porch when you visit your parents? Come on inside and I'll make you coffee."

"I can make the coffee," he said. "You go ahead and do whatever you're doing over there."

Carly went back to chopping vegetables for the chili. "You'll be more comfortable when the patio furniture arrives." Once the ingredients were all mixed together she plugged in the slow cooker, grabbed a coffee and joined Brett at the table. "The delivery truck should be here any time now. Would you be able to set up the TV for Walter when it gets here?"

"I can do that."

"Great, I'm not so good with electronics. Unless I really have to, I'd prefer to let someone else do that."

****

Walter was pleased to sit in front of his new 80" flat screen TV. Ruthie swished her bottom around, testing out her new chair. Brett filled the new freezer with the overflow of food, and Carly put the brand new sheets and blankets on her new bed. The place was buzzing with excitement and had the smell of new things in the air.

"I ain't never sat down and watched shows with you before, Walter. And I ain't never had supper cooking that I didn't fix. I hardly know what to do with myself."

"Lookit how big them fellers are on that big TV screen. I can practically see up their noses."

Carly smiled to herself as she listened to Ruthie and Walter admiring the TV. She was glad they were able to enjoy her gift to them. Well, technically it was a gift from the police protection agency. She wondered what their reaction would be when they saw the amount owing on that credit card. It was the least they could do to make up for her being kidnapped and keeping Sam away from her.

Brett poked his head in the bedroom door. "If that's all, I'd like to go home and get changed. I'll be back later."

"Yes, yes, go right ahead. Make sure you put something a little more casual on. That suit is far too stuffy for hanging around here." She handed the ties to him. "If I don't see you wearing something casual, I might have to buy you some wild floral shirts."

He took the ties from her with a troubled look. "I don't wear floral shirts, ma'am. It's not professional."

Once the bed was made, Carly stood back and admired it. She had purchased two sets of sheets, one set to be kept as a spare. There was a warm wool blanket for chilly nights. She had to have a white afghan and a patchwork quilt to make the bed look pretty. A girl should always have two new pillows so she knew whose head has been resting on them. She bought only a double bed since she would be sleeping in it alone. It was a far cry better than the old fold away bed that was now outside in the garbage pile. She could now sleep in comfort. If only she could purchase something to chase away the nightmares of being thrown in the trunk of a car.

To keep her busy in the evenings, she purchased some fabric and supplies so she could work on quilt squares. She considered buying a sewing machine but decided against it. She could quite easily appliqué by hand and sew the squares together later once she got home to her own sewing machine. She thought that would be a perfect thing to do in the evenings when she sat in the living room with Walter. She wondered if she could convince Walter to watch a movie once in a while. She would be quite content to watch cowboy movies if that was what Walter preferred.

"I think I'll make a batch of oatmeal cookies," Carly called out as she headed to the kitchen.

"I like oatmeal cookies with raisins in them," Walter said. "They go good with a cup of cocoa."

"You'll have to wait until after lunch for cocoa and cookies," Carly teased him. "I'm making grilled cheese sandwiches for lunch. Will that be agreeable with you?"

"With tomato soup, we always have grilled cheese sandwiches with tomato soup. I like my sandwich cut in soldiers."

"I think I can do that. My grandchildren like having their sandwiches cut in soldiers. Four pieces cut lengthwise. Funny that you should bring that up." The thought of her grandchildren brought a smile to her face. "I'll even let you eat it right there in front of the TV while you watch your shows. You just have to promise not to spill."

Chapter 13

The Strain of It All

She tried to cry quietly in her room, but it was not working. The sobs wracked her body, and she knew the whole house could hear her. She had tried her best to keep busy and not think about the situation but the very things she was trying to not think about were pulling her down. She missed Sam and longed to hear him call out "Honey, I'm home." She missed the phone calls from her daughter asking for advice on how to manage the 3 busy grandchildren. She missed every little thing about her own home and family. She wondered how much snow was piled up around the house and if anyone was kind enough to shovel it while they were away from home. This place didn't have any snow to shovel, heck they didn't even have grass to cut.

It was Walter who finally slipped quietly into her room and sat beside her on the bed. Surprisingly, he didn't shuffle his feet. He just sat there quietly patting her hand while she cried her heart out. She wasn't exactly sure when it happened, but she leaned her head on his shoulder, and they just sat together in silence.

"It's good to get it out," he finally said.

"I just miss my husband. I wish he were here with me."

"I know," he said soothingly. "It's just not possible right now. You have to be a brave girl and know he is in good hands. When all of this business is over, he will come for you."

"I just wish there was something I could do! All those dead bodies give me nightmares. I can't keep busy enough to take my mind off it all."

"There's nothing you can do that I can think of. You have made us all fat from the cooking you've been doing. Your pies are getting much better the more you practice. I should know I've tried all ten of 'em. If you wanner know, the apple pie was my favorite. You outdid yourself by fixing that turkey dinner. We jes usually go to Ma's Family Restaurant in town when it's turkey time."

"My mom always made the best pies. I should know how to make a good pie too. I'll get it right, I promise."

"If'n you really want something to do, I bet I could talk Ruthie into teaching you how to shoot a gun. Would you like that? That'd make Ruthie happier than a pig in mud."

"Oh, that's very kind of you but no thanks. I'm not a gun person and I could never shoot anyone."

"All right but the offer is there. If you change your mind, Ruthie'd be mighty happy to have a shootin' friend. Ain't nobody better to teach you how to shoot a gun. Now what's say we go out and watch a movie together. That'll make you feel better. We can watch that one with Scarlett and Rhett where they talk all funny like. It drives me crazy, but I know you like it. Ruthie won't say it but she likes it too. I seen her dabbing her eyes with the Kleenex last time and I didn't buy that story that she had an itchy eye."

"That sounds nice, Walter. I'd like that." Carly remembered that time very well. She had to promise to bake something special for Walter to agree to watch it. Ruthie surprised her by sniffing and dabbing her eyes. These people were growing on her.

"There's a good girl. You got Ruthie an' Brett pacin' around out there. They's so worried about you but none of them knows how to make you feel better. You're making an impression on this ol' bunch."

She stood up slowly and promised to watch the movie once she finished in the ladies room. She knew her face was puffy and red from crying. It wasn't much use to try to cover it up but she had to have a few moments alone before she faced the others.

Surprisingly, Walter's shuffle was back when he returned to his chair in the living room.

"Hot dang, Ruthie! She's gonna come an' watch a movie with us. I promised her she could watch that Gone With The Wind crap. She's been good to us so's it's the least we can do to sit through it and try not to fall asleep. You know what's wrong with that movie? It needs some of them flying monkeys like that other movie has. Needs something to liven it up a bit. All that kissing and birthing babies is enough to make me wanner puke." He made kissing noises and then sat down facing the TV.

"In that case I'm gonner make us all some popcorn." Ruthie popped up out of her chair and skipped to the kitchen.

"Some cocoa too? I like it with them little marshmallows. Got any of them candy canes left from last Christmas? They taste good when you dip 'em in the hot chocolate."

"I'll see if I can dig some up. Do you think she'll want some too? I'd do anything if it'll cheer her up. I hate the sound of that crying. Makes me wanner go out and shoot something."

When Carly settled down on the couch in the living room she was surprised to see Brett seated in a kitchen chair. He had pulled it into the living room to watch the movie with them. Even though she kept telling him to wear casual clothes he still showed up in a suit and tie. She made a mental note for her next shopping trip. Brett was going to be presented with a Hawaiian shirt and khaki pants whether he thought it professional or not. She was thinking the living room could use a comfy arm chair for guests too.

After the movie was over, they all sat in silence. The Kleenex box had been passed around to everyone in the room at some point during the movie. Walter cried when Scarlett used the curtains to make a dress. He thought that was a waste of good curtains. He made Carly chuckle.

"Oh, goodness," Carly cried. "I didn't fix anything for supper. I better get in the kitchen and get to work. What does everyone say to easy over eggs and toast. I can make some homemade chips too."

"No," Brett stunned Carly by speaking up. "I'll take everyone out for dinner. There's that new seafood restaurant in town we can try down by the waterfront. It'll be my treat."

"Hot dang!" Walter cried. "This is turning out to be a good day after all."

They all loaded into Ruthie's black charger and headed to town for dinner.

Chapter 14

It's All So Delicious

Monique and Campbell sat in the dark corner booth at the Ocean Breeze Seafood Restaurant. It was the finest restaurant on the Island of Summerview. Most diners were sitting on the patio where they could enjoy the warm weather and view of the ocean, but Monique and Campbell preferred to keep a low profile inside where they could assess any signs of danger. They didn't want anyone to overhear their conversation in case they let anything slip about their plans. Plans to modify a broken down old submarine with nuclear warheads could cause ordinary folks to ask questions.

"White Chardonnay is an excellent wine to go with your steak and lobster. The flavors make a wonderful marriage," the waiter said as he poured for them.

Monique spied Carly's group as they arrived at the restaurant. "Oh how delicious," Monique purred. "They are making this too easy for us."

Campbell turned his head to see what Monique was looking at. He didn't answer; he was too busy digging in to his dinner. "Eat your dinner while it's warm, darling. There will be plenty of time to socialize later. You don't want to be too hasty. This must be handled delicately. We don't want any mistakes. The place is full of agents."

****

"Table for four please," Brett said when they got inside. He leaned in close to the host and whispered his preference of a table along the back wall with a view of the door.

"Yes, sir," he said and whisked away to prepare a table for them.

Brett preferred to have his back to the wall so he could see everything happening in the restaurant at all times. He was not going to let anyone sneak up on him when he was in charge. It was his duty to see no harm came to Carly and he intended to see his job through.

At long last the waiter returned and beckoned the group to follow him to their table.

Their waiter's name was Dan, a young kid with a bubbly personality. He handed out menus, took their drink orders, and headed off to the bar.

"Strawberry daiquiri for the lady, tea for the senior lady, beer for the gentleman, and a chocolate milkshake for the senior gentleman."

"Oh thank you," Carly said. "This looks good."

"Will you be needing more time before you're ready to order? I can just hang out for a while and watch you from across the room. Just teasing y'all. I just can't wait to find out what y'all want to order. We have such delicious food on our menu. I love seeing happy faces eating it all up. So many people on a seafood diet around here. Get it? See food and eat it. There I go again just teasing y'all."

"Yep, I know what I want." Ruthie snapped the menu shut and looked up. "I'll have the salmon with a baked potato and Caesar salad. Walter wants the shrimp, he loves shrimp. He'll have french fries and ketchup and no salad. He don't like salad. He don't like that tartar sauce neither so don't bring any fer him. He won't eat it."

"I'll have steak and lobster," Carly said. "Can I get my steak well done. I don't like any pink coloring in my meat. I'd like the Caesar salad with that, as well, please."

"Our chef does an excellent job of cooking steaks well done."

"I believe you, but I have been served nearly raw steaks before when I specifically asked for well done."

"For you, I will personally inform the chef." He nodded his head and smiled at Carly. "We want our guests to have the best dining experience possible."

"Thank you," Carly replied. "I appreciate that."

"For the gentleman?" he looked at Brett with pen hovering over the notepad.

"Yes, I'll have the lobster, shrimp and scallops plate. No salad for me."

"Very good, you all picked some fine choices. I'll get this order to the kitchen and be right back with fresh bread for you."

"Oh I love fresh bread," said Walter. "I could eat it all up."

"Well you take it easy, make sure you leave room for your shrimp."

"Yes, Ruthie."

Carly was ordering her second daiquiri by the time the salads arrived at the table. The bread basket was nearly empty and their happy chatter filled the air.

"Well hello there, Carly. So we meet again," Monique said as she stood by their table. "We just finished our meal and thought we'd stop by and say hello."

"Monique, yes hello. I'm having dinner with my friends." She held her hand toward her table mates as she introduced Ruthie, Walter, and Brett. "Won't you join us?"

"Oh we wouldn't want to impose," she said as she grabbed two chairs for herself and Campbell to sit down.

"Monique has a very large house. It has so many levels that they even have an elevator inside. I visited her there before I came to your house, Ruthie. She has the loveliest swimming pool I have ever seen. It's called an infinity pool and it looks like water is pouring out over the edge to the rocks below."

"Campbell came into a bit of money recently and we purchased the house the minute we saw it. It is a bit on the modern side but the pool was the selling feature for me," Monique boasted happily.

"Yes," said Ruthie. "We have worked together in the past. I ain't seen the house, though."

The waiter arrived with Carly's second daiquiri and placed it in front of her. She giggled, thanked him, and immediately took a sip. "Mmmm this is delicious."

"You folks are joining this table? Can I get you anything?"

"A bottle of your best Chardonnay, please."

"Right away. The food is almost ready. I'll be bringing it to you momentarily."

"What brings you all out to this fine restaurant this evening?" Campbell asked.

"Carly here has been cooped up in the house and we wanted to treat her to a little fun," answered Walter. "I'm gonna be putting ketchup on my shrimp when it comes. It's the best. You otter try it. I might let you try one." He pointed his fork towards Monique when he made the invitation.

Carly found that to be extremely funny and giggled. Her cheeks were flushed from the daiquiris and she was enjoying herself. She didn't care anymore. She knew she was tipsy. "You know, I had a good cry earlier. I'm better now because Walter let me watch Gone with the Wind on his new 80" TV even though he didn't think

Scarlet should ruin the curtains."

Monique looked on with amusement. "An 80" TV you say. My, my, that would make a lovely view of the movie."

"I can see all my shows bigger now. If I git close enough I can see up their nose sometimes. But I don't like to do that. Who wants to see up their noses anyway?" Walter had his napkin tucked into his collar and held his knife in his left hand and fork in his right hand. He was ready to dig into his shrimp the minute the food was placed in front of him.

By the time the food arrived at the table, Carly had finished her strawberry daiquiri. "Can I get you a refill on that daiquiri, ma'am?"

"Yes please. That would be great." She giggled and leaned over to whisper in Brett's ear, but everyone could hear it. "You really should let me find you a date. I have lots of friends back home that would love to get their claws into a classy guy like you."

When the wine arrived, Monique insisted that Carly have a glass of wine too. She really wanted to help Carly let loose with all her little secrets. "It really is delicious. Just try a little bit."

Carly accepted a glass of wine. Ruthie, Walter, and Brett declined.

"You know, I would love to have you come back to the house for a visit, Carly. You and I could enjoy the pool together. It would be very relaxing. Just come for a day or two if you can spare the time, especially if you are feeling cooped up enough to cry your heart out."

"I don't know about that," said Brett. "We're kind of busy. Maybe another time."

"I would love that," slurred Carly. Three strawberry daiquiris and one glass of wine were definitely allowing her to speak freely. "I bet Ruthie and Walter would miss me but I'll make it up to them when I get back. I could make a triple layer chocolate cheese cake. I saw them make it on TV back at my house where I live. Yep, I'd do that for you." She smiled sweetly at Ruthie and Walter.

"Splendid," Monique said. "You can come home with us tonight. No need for you to bring any luggage as I am always prepared to entertain guests. I have bathing suits of every size."

"Now hold on there," Ruthie said. "The only way I'd agree to that is if Brett goes with Carly."

"That would be just fine. Campbell could use some male company."

Ruthie agreed to let Carly go with them knowing that Brett would be going too. Brett was as professional as bodyguards come, and he would not be messed with. Besides, Ruthie knew Monique and Campbell. They were secret agents too. She thought she could trust them.

Everyone said good bye in the parking lot. "You keep an eye on her, Brett. She's had too much to drink." Carly promised to return the next day after Ruthie insisted two nights away was not permissible. Carly giggled and teetered her way to Brett's car and got in the front seat. Monique wormed her way to riding with Brett and Carly. She knew Carly's lips were loose and she intended to egg her to talk during the ride to her house.

Chapter 15

Loose Lips

"Do you have a family, Carly?" Monique asked.

"Yes, I have a handsome husband named Sam but he's not here. He had to go to a funeral and take care of the widow. Oops, I don't mean it that way." Carly put her hand up to her mouth and giggled. "He's the executor of the will."

"Aww that's too bad. When will you see him again?"

"I don't know. Now he's in the police detection department or something like that. I can't remember what they call it. He's supposed to be gone for six months! I don't like him being away that long. I miss him. I miss my kids and my grandkids." Carly paused to look over her shoulder at Monique in the back seat. "I have a two-month-old grandson, you know. He's adorable," she smiled dreamily. "He smells so new, but not when he fills his diaper," she put her hand over her mouth and made a funny face. "Gosh, he doesn't smell so great then," she swished her hand in the air as if ridding the smell from the air. "I'd love to hold him in my arms right now." She knit her brows together and looked straight at Monique, "Sam bought an airplane and we were supposed to go to Las Vegas but we ended up here and I don't know where Sam is. When I get my hands on him he's gonna get an earful from me." With a heavy sigh she lifted and lowered her shoulders, "I can't wait to get home." The tears started as she whined about missing her house and her family.

Carly was saying all the things Monique had hoped she would say. Brett drove silently and didn't say a word. That suited Monique just fine. She was enjoying herself tremendously. It was all too easy. The little tramp that took Sam away from her wouldn't be so happy once Monique had her way. She intended to make Sam pay for dumping her all those years ago. His pretty little wife would be the perfect thing to get him to sink to his knees and beg forgiveness. She was just a pretty little tramp who would soon learn who was in charge.

They arrived at the house and Carly darted from the car as soon as it stopped. She headed for the nearest washroom, remembering the way from her previous visit. All those drinks were weighing her bladder down and she needed to pee something bad. Brett waited for her to come out of the washroom.

"Brett, you're a good guy! You watch out for me. Big bad guys won't get me here. Where's the party? I wanna party with my friends Monique and Campbell." Carly was well gone from the drinks.

"We're in here," Campbell called from the den. "Come on in and have another drink. I make great martinis. Come, sit down while I fix one for you."

Carly teetered over to the leather couch and plopped down on it. "I've never had a martini before. They always eat the olive in the movies. Make sure you put an extra olive in it for me. Is it like eating the marasheeeeno cherries in the fruity drinks? I love fruity drinks."

After two martinis Carly passed out cold on the couch. Brett picked her up and asked where her room was. Monique led the way to the same room that Carly stayed in the last time she was there. "We have a spare room for you too. It's on the second floor. Just below Carly's room."

"Oh no, ma'am. I'll be staying close to Carly. I'll just sleep in a chair outside her door."

"Oh how quaint. You are a keener. Nothing will happen to her here. She's safe with us. We're all agents. We can handle anything that comes our way. This house has state of the art security at our fingertips."

"Even so, I'll be sticking close to her. I have my orders."

"You're very dedicated. I wouldn't want to get in your way then. Can I bring you a blanket to keep warm?"

"No, I'll be fine. Good night, ma'am."

****

Crawling into bed with Campbell, Monique expressed her concerns over Brett. "He's going to be a tough one to get rid of, darling."

"I can handle him. You just keep the woman busy tomorrow and everything will work out smoothly."

"Is the submarine ready?"

"Nearly ready. They moved it into position. We're waiting for some special parts. I have some master technicians arriving soon. Everything has to be perfect for our plan to work. You and I will have the world at our fingertips. It's all coming together."

Monique got up and stood at the end of the bed. "I love your devious mind. You deserve a little fun time." She licked his toes and then did a strip tease for Campbell. Then they wiggled under the covers hungrily groping each other.

Chapter 16

Hangover

At 2:00 am Carly woke up, tiptoed to the door and peeked out. Brett sat sleeping in a chair so she poked him. "Wake up, Brett. I want to go for a swim."

Brett opened his eyes and stood immediately. "It's late; you should wait until tomorrow to go for a swim. Your hosts are in bed, you don't want to wake them. Besides the security alarms are all set. Go back to bed and get some sleep."

"Oh, you're a spoil sport. Always the perfect gentleman. I like that." Carly returned to bed and slept until morning.

****

"Good morning, sleepy head." Monique pulled the curtains open and let the sunshine pour into the room.

Carly groaned and put a hand to her head. "My head hurts."

"Somebody drank a little too much last night. You get yourself out of that bed and showered. When you come down for breakfast, we'll see about getting you a bloody mary. They're the best thing for hangovers. Then you can lounge by the pool all day."

"Lounging by the pool does sound nice. I think I'll opt out of the bloody mary and have a simple glass of orange juice."

Outfitted in bathing suit and robe, she made her way out the back door of the house and down the stairs towards the pool house. It was a steep staircase down a hill lush with shrubbery. There was comfy rattan furniture with luxurious pillows inside the pool house but Carly decided to park herself on the lounge chair outside on the pool deck. There was a white sun hat on the lounge chair that she put on, slipped the flip flops off her feet and sank into the well-padded chair. She lay back and enjoyed the warmth of the sun. When she left home it was on the verge of winter but here it was heavenly summer.

Brett arrived poolside right after her, still dressed in his black suit. "You really should see Campbell about borrowing some swim trunks. Take it easy and enjoy yourself."

"I'm on duty, ma'am. Work before pleasure."

"Oh phooey! You can do your job and relax too."

The infinity pool seemed to blend in with the lovely view. The blue sky, palm trees and rich green foliage disappeared down towards the ocean. There was a faint shadow of the mountains in the distance. The air smelled warm and the surroundings felt peaceful. Carly slipped into the pool and splashed about. She tried to send a big splash in Brett's direction but he ducked back and she missed.
She dove under water and swam to the deep end then swam a few lengths of the pool. All activity caused her head to throb so she decided to lounge quietly by the pool for the rest of the day.

Climbing out of the pool, she grabbed a towel to dry off. Monique was coming towards her with a fruity drink. "I thought you might enjoy a mai tai drink. I remember you saying you like the fruity drinks."

"Oh thank you," she said taking the drink and heading back to the lounge chair. She placed the drink on the table beside the chair but didn't intend to drink it. She had done enough drinking the night before and didn't intend to add to her pounding headache. She got her boo hoo's out of her system and was ready to face her fate head on.

"Campbell has finally convinced Brett to change into swim trunks. They'll be coming back to swim shortly. The dear man really is dedicated to looking out for you. It took a bit of convincing, I must say."

Carly lay back in the lounge chair and drifted off to sleep. She woke much later to the sounds of splashing as Brett and Campbell swam lengths. Carly was pleased to see Brett finally toning down the bodyguard image.

"Look at you," Monique said. "You are red from the sun. Best get you inside and put something on to ease that sunburn." The two women headed up the steps to the house.

"You have such a lovely place here. I can't get over the fantastic view. I thank you for inviting me here today."

"You know we have a yacht too. Maybe we can take you out there today. You would love it."

"I don't know I really should get back to Ruthie and Walter. Maybe we can go there another time with you."

"I insist you see our yacht today. It won't take but a quick call to Ruthie and I promise I will have you back to her by nightfall. You go and get changed while I make the phone call."

Carly did as she was told. She was thrilled to inspect the selection of clothes. She chose a pair of red Capri's, red and white boat shirt, and white sneakers. She pulled her hair into a pony tail in case it was windy on the water and grabbed a navy blue windbreaker on her way out the door.

"Ah there you are. You look perfect. There is a cab waiting for us downstairs so let's go." Monique hurried Carly along.

"What about Brett? Is he coming with us?"

"Ah yeah, Brett said he couldn't come along with us. Something about getting seasick, the poor dear. He said he'll see you back at Ruthie's house later tonight. Campbell will be along in a minute or so. He just has some loose ends to tie up. We'll wait for him in the cab."

"Oh," Carly said. "I haven't had very good luck with cabs lately. I sure hope this cab ride will be much more pleasant than the last two rides."

They weren't sitting in the cab for long before Campbell came dashing out of the house, got in the cab and they sped away.

Chapter 17

Ticking Time Bomb

Ruthie and Walter pulled up in front of Monique and Campbell's house. Ruthie got out of the car and told Walter to wait where he was. She had a funny feeling and wanted to make sure the coast was clear before she allowed Walter to follow her. The place seemed deserted as Ruthie made her way up the three flights of stairs to the front door. The square modern design of this house was not to her taste. The place had glass balconies everywhere you looked. The front door was open so she stepped inside.

"Hello," she called. No answer. Red flags were going up in Ruthie's mind. She stepped further inside and called out again. She heard muffled sounds and climbed the spiral staircase until she found Brett on the first landing in front of the elevator door. He was tied in a chair with duct tape over his mouth. Ruthie's eyes popped open wide when she saw the bomb that was attached to his feet with the time displayed twenty-five minutes and counting.

"You hold on there just a minute," she said to Brett. "This here is a job for Walter. Nobody knows how to defuse a bomb like ol Walter. I'll go get him and be right back."

Her feet hadn't carried her so fast in ages. She was winded by the time she reached Walter in the car.

"Brett," she stopped to catch her breath. "Brett's inside," huff, huff, "and he's tied up with a bomb attached to his foot. We need you to come quick."

"Jumpin' Jiminies," Walter snapped to full alert and got out of the car. It had been a long time since he felt needed and he was happy to be of assistance. "Get my case outta the trunk of the car and bring it along. You better tell me what the thing looks like."

"You want me to tell you what your tool case looks like?"

"No, gall dang it woman, I need you to tell me what the bomb looks like!"

"Oh, yeah, that. Well it's black and it said twenty-five minutes on the clock."

"Twenty-five minutes! We better get a move on." Walter's feet weren't doing the usual shuffle. He was able to climb the steps one at a time. By the time he reached the top of the three flights outside, it was his turn to be winded.

"There's an elevator in this place that'll take us right to Brett. Come on, you can rest on the ride up."

While they waited for the elevator door to open Walter started talking out the possible scenarios. "We gotter decide if it's a kid type bomb or a bad bomb. Them kids learn how to make dry ice bombs, chemical bombs, and firework bombs. They see these things in movies and don't bother listening to the part that tells 'em not to try this at home." He shook his head and continued on, "Nah, if it were one of them it'd be blowed up by now. Besides, I know what Campbell's capable of. I did teach him everything he knows. That dang fool'll likely try something that he thinks'll trip me up. That ain't gonner happen. He used to be fond of them pipe bombs. Oh how I miss the good old days. Don't you worry none, Ruthie, I still got it all up in my noggin'."

The elevator door opened and they stepped inside. "Nowadays them bomb squads have those new robots they can send in to defuse the bomb. I saw one in action one time on a TV program and it was pretty spiffy. All the bomb techs was wearing bomb suits and blast shields. They had rope devices and hotsticks too. I never had none of that modern technology in my day. Sure woulda made things easier."

Ruthie was sweating from the danger of the whole situation. She wished the elevator could move faster. Didn't the dang thing know there was a bomb attached to Brett's leg and that they were all minutes away from being blown to smithereens? When the elevator door finally slid open she could see that Brett was even more worried than she was. The sweat was dripping down his face. "You sit tight there Brett. Walter's here. Just as soon as we get this ol' bomb defused we'll git that duct tape off yer face and git you untied. Did Campbell give any clues about the bomb before he left you like this? Walter'll need to know everything you can tell us."

Brett shook his head back and forth and made some mumbling sounds that nobody could understand.

"OK Ruthie, I need you to open my tool case and find the wire cutters and splicer."

Ruthie dropped the heavy black tool case on the floor with a thud. She got down on her knees and opened the lid. She stared at all the tools for a bit before saying, "What's a wire cutter and splicer look like?"

"You got your hand on the wire cutter right there, peaches. Just hand that to me fer now. It'll do just fine." He looked into Brett's eyes and assured him, "we got fifteen minutes, sonny, plenty of time. Don't you worry none. Walter's here. Normally I'd recommend someone to call 9-1-1 in a situation like this but I'm in charge now with no time to spare. This is the very stuff I was trained to do in my military days. Everything we need is all right here in front of us."

Walter gently removed the front cover of the bomb and sat back to look it over. "We just gotter cut the wire leads to the primer and then the reactor wire. That'll stop the ignition timer and we'll all sit back and heave a sigh of relief."

Ruthie was busy trying to calm her heart pounding in her chest when she realized that Walter just called her peaches. He hadn't called her peaches in years and she kind of liked hearing it again. She watched Walter in amazement working away like he was a spry young man again. He was so focused and in tune with his faculties. She sure hoped he had enough energy to pull this off. She looked around the spiral staircase encased in nothing but glass windows for three stories. If the bomb went off, they were all going to go sailing through those glass windows.

"We're counting on you to get us through this, Walter." Ruthie said keeping her eyes glued to the timer which now showed five minutes remaining.

"A little snip here, and a little snip there," he worked quickly to snip as he spoke, "and voila! We're all set." He put a hand on Brett's shoulder to offer comfort that all was under control. "Let's get this young man out to the car and outer this place."

Ruthie didn't stop to question Walter, she grabbed a swiss army knife from the tool box and cut the ropes, freeing Brett's hands. Brett ripped the duct tape off his mouth and said, "We gotta get out of here fast. One thing Campbell did say is that he added a second bomb to go off once the first one was defused."

Brett grabbed Walter in a fireman carry, throwing the old man over his shoulders, and flew down the stairs with Ruthie right behind him. They piled into the car as fast as they could with Brett taking the wheel. He floored the car to get away from the imminent explosion. Walter sat in the backseat with Ruthie lying down across the seat, huffing and puffing. She had never run that fast in her life. Walter was proud of her for keeping up with Brett. They heard the explosion and Brett stopped the car to look back and see the cloud of smoke rising.

"Sorry I left your tool box behind there, Walter." Ruthie said.

"Tools can be replaced, my dear. I'm just glad we all got out together, alive."

Chapter 18

Carly's M.I.A.

The car came to a stop in front of Ruthie and Walter's house. Nobody moved. They all sat in silence.

Ruthie broke the silence first. "We came to get you because we got a message from headquarters. The double agents were identified as Monique and Campbell. They're heavily involved in the Thor's Hammer scheme. They financed the terrorist group to steal an abandoned nuclear submarine and rig it to blow up."

"Too bad you couldn't have come earlier," Brett said. "They took Mrs. Davenport with them. It's my entire fault because I let Campbell convince me to go for a swim. I knew I shouldn't do it but now it's done and I'm to blame."

"Hog wash!" Walter declared getting out of the car. "Them two had you wrapped up in their scheme and it's nobody's fault but theirs. I'm going inside to get me some cookies. All this spy work made me hungry. Foller me if'n you want some cookies too."

****

Inside the house Ruthie told Walter to go sit in his chair in front of the TV. She'd make up a snack for everyone. Brett followed Walter into the living room and sat on the couch. Ruthie fussed around in the kitchen banging dishes and cupboard doors as she worked. Finally she brought out a platter of chicken sandwiches, cheese, crackers, and fresh fruit.

"How come everybody's so gloomy? Turn the TV on so's we can watch something while we eat."

Walter picked up the remote and turned the TV on and flipped through the channels. He was feeling sentimental remembering when Carly told him she bought him an 80" TV. He stopped flipping channels when he came upon a cooking show.

"Whatcha stopping on that old cooking show fer, Walter?"

"Aww Ruthie, I miss Carly and I just know if she was here with us she'd a gone and hollered to stop flipping through the dang channels cuz she wanted to see what they was cooking today. Look at that, they's making up one of them cheese cakes she's always talking about. I'm gonner watch it so's I can tell her how to make it when she comes back to us."

The gloom could be felt by all three of them. Silently they all remembered the things Carly did and wished she could be there with them. At the time they may have thought she was a teensy tiny bit annoying but they'd sure give their right arms to hear her clanking away in the kitchen.

"Well," Brett broke the silence. "I better make a phone call to Commander Steele and let him know Carly's missing in action. It's best I get it over with now and face the consequences."

When Brett excused himself to make the call, Ruthie thought she'd take a look in Carly's room and see if it needed straightening up. Entering the room slowly, the smell of Carly's perfume wafted up her nose. She remembered complaining about the smell until Carly burst into tears and told her that perfume was the exact perfume her own momma wore and that it comforted her. Ruthie backed off knowing Carly needed to be allowed some space to deal with all the stresses she had been through since she left her quiet home to be in the middle of this craziness. Now she found herself tempted to dab some of that perfume on her own wrist to keep Carly's memory close to her.

The bed did not need making as Carly had the place looking like a show room. A thick pink and white patchwork quilt was looking so pretty with matching pillows propped on top. There was a little pink heart pillow leaning against the big pillows. A white afghan was folded neatly and hung over the ladder-back chair sitting next to the bed. She had 3 romance novels neatly stacked on top of a crossword puzzle magazine on the chair. Hanging in the closet there were newly purchased baby clothes with the tags still attached. Airplanes adorned the sleepers. There was a t-shirt with the letter "C" on the front, likely intended for the older grandson and a pretty purple sundress for the granddaughter. Ruthie smiled at how much shopping Carly had squeezed out of that credit card the government had given her. Her nose started running so she left the room in search of a tissue.

"I heard that," Walter hollered. "You're getting all emotional from being in her room."

"I ain't emotional. It's her dang perfume stuffing up my nose. I knew there'd be trouble when she started spraying that infernal stuff around the place."

Walter smiled to himself because he knew his Ruthie. If she didn't like that perfume she'd have grabbed it outta that room and tossed it outside. His wife never minced words before. If she let the perfume stay it meant she was getting soft. He knew she grew attached to Carly and there was no way he was letting her deny it.

 When Ruthie returned to the living room she started collecting the dishes left from the snack they had all eaten together. She went into the kitchen and saw Brett through the window. He was outside pacing back and forth in the yard talking on his cell phone. "I wonder how that phone call is going," Ruthie said to Walter.

"I don't know fer sure but he's gonna wear a ditch in our front yard with all that pacing he's doing."

Ruthie sat down hard in her chair beside Walter. "How could we have let this happen, Walter? I wish I never let her go and stay at that place in the first place."

"Now, now. We didn't know then what we know now. Them two agents is just devils in disguise. They was just waiting for the opportunity to steal her away from us. They's just up to no good and there ain't no other way to say it!"

"Where did we go wrong with them? I trained Monique myself. You had a hand in training Campbell. We turned out some darn good agents over the years. None of 'em ever turned bad. They're all like my own kids I never had. I think I'm gonner go out back and do some target practice."

Walter patted Ruthie's hand. "You go do that. It'll make you feel better." He watched Ruthie stand and shuffle to the back of the house. He heard the screen door slam and then the shooting began.

Chapter 19

Sam Gets the News

The Intelligence team was surveying the suspected hiding spot of the refurbished nuclear submarine dubbed Thor's Hammer. The deployed soldiers were using electronic sensors to gather information from a distance without being observed. Now that they knew the exact location of the submarine they could report back to Commander Steele. Once the intelligence personnel had time to analyze the findings, Commander Steele would formulate the battle plan.

Sam paced his room knowing the team was searching for the sub. As soon as the Commander gave the word he knew he was going in and the chances of coming out alive were pretty slim. It was his job to put a stop to this plan of mass destruction. He would do it at all costs in order to save innocent lives. This was by far the most danger he had ever faced.

He pulled out a picture of his wife and family. He kept it in his shirt pocket close to his heart. "Hang in there, babe. This will all be over soon enough and you can go back home safe and sound. I sure hope I'll be going home with you." He longed to vacation with her on a beach somewhere with nothing better to do than enjoy each other with no interruptions.

When his cell phone rang he quickly tucked the photo back in his shirt pocket. This was the call he had been waiting for. He headed out the door to the Command Headquarters for the briefing and instructions.

****

The news that Carly was missing hit Sam like a ton of bricks. There was no doubt in his mind that he would find her and get her out of there. When he had Carly somewhere safe he was going to have words with the Dave crew for handling this whole thing like a bunch of twits. Why on earth would Ruthie and Walter allow Carly to go off with Monique and Campbell? His anger was rising the more he thought about it all. He slammed his fist down on the table sending causing coffee cups to topple over and spill.

"Hey, settle down there. You need to calm down and think this through. Use your brain and not your brawn right now. If you can't handle your emotions we'll pull your ass off this mission and let the professionals handle it."

Looking around the room at all the concerned faces, Sam sat back in his chair and promised to calm down. The last thing he wanted to happen was to be pulled off the mission. "Sorry about that, I'll be fine from here on in." He looked at his feet for a moment before looking up and declaring, "I'm the only professional you need for this job."

Commander Steele glared at Sam before he continued to explain the slide presentation. Sam watched through brooding eyes. He could not find any reason why Monique and Campbell would fund a terrorist group to upgrade a rotting nuclear submarine. How did they get involved with a terrorist group? How did they get enough money to fund such a huge project? What was their ultimate purpose and why the hell did they kidnap his wife?

Sam worked with Monique many years ago. She was a good agent, knew her stuff. They'd even had a little fling which now made Sam's skin crawl at the thought of it. She was on the wild side which appealed to Sam at the time. He had been a single man with no intentions of ever being tied down. Back then he enjoyed the attention from the ladies, lots of different ladies.

Once he met Carly he forgot all about Monique. Carly was like sunshine and roses. Her smile made him weak in the knees. He had never met anyone that made him swoon and get tongue-tied before. He knew life would never be the same again once Carly entered his world. After three dates he asked her to marry him. He remembered being wildly ecstatic when she said yes. She was his soul mate and he would do anything to take care of her.

Tuning back in to the briefing, Sam listened intently as they described the nuclear submarine dubbed Thor's Hammer. "This thing was left rotting in the Soviet submarine graveyard on the Kola Peninsula. No less than seven active missiles still on board and intact. They could create thunder like Thor's hammer once released. These missiles are designed to go off, when they reach a certain altitude they break apart and seven missiles are released from each warhead. They surround the target with total devastation. Much like marching around the walls of Jericho until the walls came tumbling down. Except this baby could do it in an instant."

The group watched the next set of slides showing the terrorist group working under the guise of a scrap collection crew. They towed the decaying sub to a hidden cave where they turned it into a shining vessel ready for its first mission.

"Surveillance equipment picked up conversations about successfully rigging this sub to have remote control capabilities. They don't intend to be on board. They intend to place it on location and destroy it when the mission is complete. The time and place of this is still unknown to us but our sources tell us they believe there has been unusual activity in some remote caves off the Coast of Summerview Island in the South Pacific."

Pictures of various individuals were displayed next. "Dmitri Deklumkova has been eliminated. He attempted to kidnap Mrs. Carly Davenport and was stopped by Agent Ruth Green. Dmitri has been connected with a terrorist group called Brothers of Mayhem. They get involved in causes that pay them enough money. These guys are deadly killers and think murdering their victims is child's play. It is recommended you use extreme caution if you come in contact with any member of this group. Act first and ask questions later are the best policy. Dmitri has three brothers whose whereabouts are unknown. Alexi, Sergei, and Yuri. They are big and mean buggers. Now that their brother is dead they will be out for blood."

Next up were pictures of Monique and Campbell. "These two

agents are believed to be at the center of this scheme. They have both been active with this organization and have inside information about this mission. Yesterday it was reported to us that they have taken Mrs. Davenport with them and they have not been heard from since."

A photo was shown of the demolished house where Monique and Campbell left Brett tied up.

"Agent Brett Delany was in charge as Mrs. Davenport's bodyguard but they left him behind tied to a bomb. Lucky for us Agent Walter Green was able to defuse the bomb. Agents Brett, Ruth, and Walter managed to escape before a second bomb was triggered and exploded leaving the house in pieces."

A photo of a smiling Carly was shown next.

"Please be advised that Mrs. Davenport has no knowledge of Operation Walls of Jericho. She was left in top secret protective custody in case she became a target of kidnapping in order to bring down her husband, Agent Sam Davenport. It is unknown to us at this time what knowledge she may have of this mission. She was first told she was going to fly to Las Vegas in an airplane that Sam and the Dave crew bought and refurbished. After her tangle with Dmitri Deklumkova she was then told Sam was taken into police protection for walking into a bank robbery. Please use extreme caution if you are fortunate to rescue her. She may be confused and in need of delicate diplomacy."

An aerial view of Ruthie and Walter's property was shown next.

"Headquarters will be re-established at the home of Agents Ruthie and Walter Green. All available agents will relocate there effective immediately. Ladies and gentlemen, you are dismissed."

Chapter 20

Catching Up with Old Friends

He couldn't report in to Headquarters until he had a private visit with Ruthie and Walter. The old place still looked the same. Barbed wire fence at the entrance to the property still concealed gun turrets. The welcome mat no doubt still concealed a trap door for unwelcome guests to fall through.

He had spent a lot of time here when he was training. Walter was the best instructor around when it came to demolition techniques and Ruthie had taught him how to hit a bull's eye with his eyes closed. Not only were they qualified instructors, they managed to squirm their way into his heart. No matter how homesick he got they always made him laugh with their quirky behavior. He didn't know of any trainees that came away from this place without being considered family.

Standing quietly in the front hall he looked around. They never could keep him from getting inside the house undetected. A wonderful aroma was coming from the empty kitchen. To his right he saw Walter sitting in front of the largest TV he'd ever seen. "Holy Cow," he said, and then whistled. "How on earth did you get a TV that large in this little old house? No wonder you didn't know I was here. "

Walter looked up in surprise. He stood and shuffled over to give Sam a handshake and then the two men embraced. "It's good to see you, Sam. Ruthie's awfully upset with herself for losing your wife. Don't be too hard on her. I ain't seen her cry in years."

"I could never be mad at Ruthie!" The two men went into the living room and sat down. "I know those double agents brought this trouble on. It couldn't be helped. I just wish I could get my hands on those scoundrels. I have to stay professional or I'll be removed from the case."

Ruthie came into the room and caught sight of Sam. She rushed to hug him. "Oh Sam! I lost your wife and I'm so sorry. She was the sweetest thing ever and I let you down."

"I was just telling Walter here that those scoundrel double agents are to blame for this. It wasn't your fault. Don't you worry, we're all here now and we'll bring her back safe and sound, together. She's too good a cook to let them get away with this."

"Oh man you just spoke a mouthful," Walter chuckled at the memories. "Once she started feeling better she didn't stop cooking for us. We had cookies and turkey dinners and man oh man I can't tell you what all she cooked up fer us. She made a different kinda pie every day." He rubbed his tummy. "They was pumpkin and blueberry and apple. I like blueberry the best but it sure makes yer poop turn all black." He waved his hand in the air as if to wipe that thought away. "She said her momma made the best pies and if she had so much time on her hands then she was gonna leave here knowin' how to make a proper pie." Walter's eyes lit up and he continued, "them pies got better every day. They tasted good too. At first there was flour ever which way on the floor and ceiling." He gestured to the ceiling, "she got better at cleaning after herself too. Now that she's gone, Ruthie's taken up to cooking some of her recipes. She's got a beef stew cooking in that slow cooker she bought right now." Walter sniffed the air, "it sure smells good too. Ruthie never was much on cooking and working in the kitchen." He stopped to think a moment. "Your Carly sure turned our old house around. She even bought me a 80" TV so's I can see my programs better. Now you tell me if you can't see up them guys noses." Walter leaned toward the television and demonstrated looking up at the images on the screen. "An' she bought Ruthie that chair you's sittin in right now. Just wait till you see the spare room. You won't recognize it, she got it fixed up all fancy and pink and all. Ruthie goes in there a lot just to smell her perfume."

"Aww you stop that now." Ruthie pointed a finger at Walter. "I told ya I'm allergic to that perfume. It makes my nose all runny and I get boogers dripping ever which way that I gotta run fer tissues."

She pulled a tissue out of her pocket to show Walter and Sam. "Then my dang eyes git all red and swell up. It don't make me cry, it jes makes me allergic is all. Kinda like crying when I cut onions." She waved her hand in the air, "if you wanner call that cryin' then I guess I was cryin'."

"That's what you always say, woman. I know better. Ain't nothing wrong with crying once in a while. Let yer emotions all out or you'll turn cranky like me. Now me for instance, I cry all the time when them folks get the answers wrong on my game shows. If I know the answers they should know 'em too. I ain't no rocket scientist but I know a few things once in a while."

Sam sat back and enjoyed the bantering. This was the best part of Ruthie and Walter. He sure missed this quirky couple. It was then he saw the fabric and sewing supplies sitting in the corner by the couch. "Is this Carly's handiwork?"

"Aw shucks, I fergot about that." Walter paused for a moment as the emotion flushed his face. "It's been sitting there since the last time she worked on it. We was watching Gone With The Wind to cheer her up. She'd been crying something terrible so I said she could come an' watch that movie on my new TV. She called it applique, and said she was going to make it into a quilt when she got home." Walter brushed off the emotions and returned to his playful self to say, "She sure poked her fingers an awful lot. Surprising she didn't get blood ever which where." He shook his head and rubbed his fingers as though he were wiping blood away. "It sure was good to watch her putting it all together. She calls that Sunbonnet Sue and Overall Sam. You wouldn't see the likes of me with some girlie covers on my bed. Ruthie says she likes it though. Don't know why she don't call it Sunbonnet Carly since you get to be Overall Sam."

"Were you able to cheer her up?"

"Oh yeah we sure did. She and Ruthie were blubbering up a storm from the movie. Then when it was over Brett took us all out to that Seafood place in town for a fancy supper. I had my favorite shrimps with ketchup. It don't get any better than that kinda stuff. Carly got to drinkin' a couple of them fancy drinks and she was happier than a cookie at Christmas. Sure was nice to see her smile again. All we'd seen up to that point was worry lines all over her face. Except when we got this here TV all set up. She smiled real perty then."

"I'm glad you two took such good care of her. Commander Steele made the right decision to have her stay here with you. I'm only sorry I didn't think of it myself before he did. "

"Aw now don't go gitting all emotional, Sam. You'll git Ruthie crying all over again. Any treasure of yours is a treasure to us. We'll git her back safe and sound. Don't you worry none. Say, you should see her room. She went shopping with that credit card the government gave her. She had a great time shopping too, I might add. Anyway, she bought the cutest things for those grandbabies of yers. Go on in and take a look."

Sam went into the bedroom and had a look around. He melted at the smell her perfume. The furniture may have been different than they had at home but he could see Carly's touch in every little detail. He felt her presence in this room and it made him want to curl up like a baby and feel close to her. It made him want to get her back all the more. "I'll find you Carly and I'll bring you home safe and sound."

Chapter 21

Headquarters Relocated

After visiting and having dinner with his old friends, he was feeling motivated to get back to work. Sam went out the front door and around to the side of the house to the basement cellar entrance. He opened the doors and walked down the stairs. The huge underground headquarters was bustling with activity. He saw Commander Steele in the back office and headed in that direction.

"Good to see you, Sam. We have our scout teams searching for the sub. We're combing Summerview Island. If it's anywhere around there, we'll find it."

"While we're waiting for them to find the sub, I'd like to go to the scene of the bombing. There may be some clues I can pick up on. I want to take Brett and Walter with me. They can walk me through the scene."

"That sounds fine. You won't need your Arctic gear here. This weather system is more to my liking, I must say. I do miss my floor to ceiling stone fireplace back in Tuk, though."

"You won't hear any complaints from me about 76 degree Fahrenheit weather in November."

Ruthie insisted on coming along. She wanted to do the driving, but Sam convinced her to let him take the wheel. They all piled into the shiny new black charger and hit the road.

"I think we're being followed," Sam said not long after they had driven down the highway. "You better buckle up your seatbelts and hold on tight." Sam stepped on the gas, squealed the tires and tore the road up in an effort to get away. The green car kept pace with him. Sam slowed down, watching in his rearview mirror the whole time. The green car slowed as well.

"There's a park up ahead to the right," Brett pointed. "You can pull in there. We'll show you one of the features the Dave crew installed in this baby." Brett pushed a button on the dash of the car and a round black device dropped to the ground underneath the car. "Drive over to that clump of trees and park facing the road." When they were parked Brett pushed another button which caused the charger to be covered. "We are now disguised as a holographic clump of trees. Nobody will ever know we are hiding in here." Brett paused, noting Sam's raised eyebrows. "We have a clear view of the tracking device that we dropped on the road. When the green car drives by I'll activate it to attach itself magnetically to the underbelly of the car and we'll be able to monitor their whereabouts. We'll be able to hear their conversations too. Ruthie has the controls to monitor them in the back seat. The device can also be monitored by headquarters."

They all watched the green car drive by their hiding spot. The device attached to the car effortlessly and noiselessly. The green car slowed and turned around. After it was gone, Brett disengaged their hiding device and Sam drove back to the highway.

"They are driving to town," Ruthie said. "I'll monitor their activities from the car when you two go check out the bomb site. Walter can fill you in on what you need to know about the bomb when you get back here. I reckon he'd never be able to walk through all that mess. He don't walk too good as it is."

Brett directed Sam to where the house used to be. They parked as close as they could and walked the rest of the way up to the rubble. There wasn't much of a structure left. The bomb did a thorough job of destroying it all.

"This used to be a four story modern design house." Brett pointed things out as he led the way. "It had several glass balconies and an underground garage. It had three sets of five steps up to the main floor." He paused a moment, turning to Sam, "The elevator inside the house was in a spiral staircase that was encased in glass." Kneeling down, he carefully picked up a shard of glass. "They must not be worried about money to just blow the place up like that."

"This place has a killer view of the ocean." Sam shielded his eyes from the sun as he took in the view. "The sun makes that water sparkle." He looked around the whole lot. "It does seem a pity to destroy it."

Back in the car, Sam asked Walter if he thought Campbell was making the same old bombs or if he had learned any new skills.

"The bomb looked the same as always so I was perty shocked when Brett said there was a second bomb gonna go off. It's not all that original but I gotta hand it to him for tricking me."

"Next stop, town," Sam said. "I'm going shopping while Brett asks questions around town. Find out if anyone's seen Monique and Campbell in town. Maybe somebody's heard them talking."

****

Sam placed his shopping bags in the trunk of the car and closed it when Brett came back from his visit with the locals. Both men got in the car to compare notes in private.

"Headquarters has sent a team to check out the green car. They're gonna follow them around and find out what they're up to," said Ruthie.

"Some of the folks I talked to recognized Monique and Campbell from the picture I showed them," said Brett. "They were regulars at the Seafood Restaurant. After dinner they often went to the Marina or Rock Mountain Lookout. Everyone just thought they were a cute couple in love."

"We'll need to get a team out to investigate the Marina and Rock Mountain Lookout."

"I'm on it, Sam. I'm sending a message to Headquarters right now."

"Good job, Ruthie. Does this car have any other little features I should know about?"

"It has off-roading capabilities for one thing. Not to mention it has great air time when you jump over things. You kind of have to try it out to believe it. The jet rocket boosters make it spectacular."

"Well, Brett. I think we will have to go on a training mission right now. I never could pass up an opportunity to go off-roading and off-grounding. Yee Hawww!"

Chapter 22

Walter's Lab and House Security

"OK Walter. It's time for you to give me a tour of your lab. I want to see everything you've been up to since I last saw you."

Walter looked at Sam with innocence. "Who, me? I ain't been up to nothin special. I'm just an old guy who cain't keep up no more. That dang Campbell went and outsmarted me and I don't like it. It burns my undies something fierce!"

"Well, old man. You gonna sit there and belly ache about the things you can't do or are you going to show me your latest experiments?"

"I thought you'd never ask, Sam. Me an' that Dave crew been havin lots of fun with our new trainees. Seeing's how that Thor's Hammer's loaded with seven nuclear missiles that open up to havin' seven more bombs inside each one, we been practicin on simulators to learn how to shut it down. We also been experimentin with robotics so's we can do some remote control toys of our own."

Brett, Sam, and Ruthie followed Walter as he shuffled into the living room and sat himself down in front of his TV. "Now don't you go tellin' Carly none of this but we hooked up lots of video equipment so I can see what's goin on ever which way 'round this place. Ain't gonna be a mouse scurry through the field that I don't know about." He turned on the TV and demonstrated the various screens he had at his finger tips.

"I cain't get around the place too good no more now that I got a little old but I can sure watch everything that's goin on from this here chair. See here, at the back of the property we got old junkers we hauled in from the dump. Nobody else wants 'em but we sure like to play with 'em. They's loaded down with explosives. Ever now an' then we blow 'em up good and try out new ways to do it."

Sam leaned his head in closer to have a better look. "You've got at least a dozen old vehicles there. Cars, trucks, buses, ambulances, a sea crate."

"Yeah, it's the best fun. The Agency spared no expenses when it came to training up them young fellers. We have fun thinking up new ways to make a boom. We do things like fireworks, gun powder trails, fire crackers, sticks of dynamite, barrels of gasoline, barrels of oil, everything we can think of to teach and learn the latest about explosives. Of course, we got the place rigged so's nobody can sneak in and get hurt. Safety is our main priority while we's experimenting and training. Course there ain't nobody around here for miles so we're in a good place to practice." He paused to scratch his head. "I wonder sometimes, if'n we should teach them fellers how to cook so's things don't burn and explode." He nodded his head thoughtfully. "Ever trainee otter know how to cook a meal too, ya know."

"How come I haven't seen any of the Dave crew since I got here?"

"Oh, they's scared of you. They think you'll get mad at them for losing Carly. We all feel perty bad about that. So instead they've got their heads together thinking up gadgets to help find her."

"You still got the obstacle course back there?"

"You bet we do. We got it all set up so's I can watch the course and change targets to heighten the learning value to the trainees as they run through it. We even got a driving range for them to learn how to drive properly in high speed chases. I got it all right here at my fingertips."

"How about security? You got cameras everywhere but what do you have that'll keep the place safe against attacks?"

"You know we got them gun towers at the entrance. We got protection walls that come up outta the ground to hide and protect the house. Heck we got a whole army underground in the headquarters. When the warning alarms are set off this place'll come alive. Headquarters has some secrets of their own. We got cameras pointed every direction you can think of. Anyone tries to sneak up on us we'll see 'em coming for miles. If'n they do sneak in here somehow, we got miles of property here that they won't be able to find their way around. We'll have 'em so lost they'll be sorry they come sneaking around."

"I'm going to have to take a tour of your driving range with Ruthie's car. I could use some brushing up on my skills."

"Sounds good to me, Sam. Take Brett with you. He knows the place like the back of his hand. He knows all the ins and outs of that car, too. Make sure you wear the headsets so's we can communicate."

"Come on, Ruthie. We's gonna get some fun to watch on the training courses. We should have a snack while we watch. We got time while Sam and Brett get ready."

"Good idea, Walter. How about some grapes and apple slices with cheese?"

"Crackers and peanut butter too! I got a hankering for some peanut butter. We got any of that soda pop in the fridge? I'd like some cold soda pop."

"Soda pop's gonna give you gas. Why don't you have some apple juice instead?"

"Aw, come on now. This here's a special treat. I want that green lime soda pop. It's my favorite. You better hurry, them boys is just about there. We don't wanner miss any of the fun."

Chapter 23

Green Car Returns

The warning alarms went off at 2:00 am. Sam was asleep on the couch, snuggled under his new red plaid blankets. He bounced up ready for action. Brett ran in from the porch. Ruthie and Walter shuffled out of their bedroom and turned on the video surveillance screens to see where the threat was coming from. They all stared in amazement as the flashing screen showed a green car driving slowly down the highway towards the property.

"It's that green car that was following us when we went to inspect the bombed-out house. We put a bug on it so how come nobody told us it was in the area before now?"

"Can you zoom in and get a closer look at it?" Sam asked while he pulled out his cell phone. "I'll call headquarters and see if they are watching this too."

Walter zoomed in as requested. There was no driver behind the wheel. "I don't like the looks of this," said Walter. "A moving car with no driver can only mean they got it rigged with robotics." He started flipping switches. "I got a funny feeling about this so's I'm putting up the spikes along the driveway in case it drives in here. I'm putting up the security wall to protect the house.

"Headquarters tells me they have not had any readings on the bug we placed on the green car for several hours. They are definitely not getting any readings that it's in our vicinity. They're sending a team up to intercept it."

Everyone watched the screens as Walter showed the spikes being raised in the driveway. "Those spikes oughta slow 'em down. We're not playing tiddly winks with them babies."

Next Walter raised the security wall. The ground in front of the porch shook as it emerged from the soil and rose several feet higher than the house. "You never know when you'll need a little privacy from nosy neighbors." He chuckled at his own joke. "Bullet proof and strong enough to fend off a Sherman tank smashing into it." Then he showed screens where two more walls rose from the earth on either side of the big wall. They were placed slightly ahead on either side of the big wall.

"Just cause I got a funny feeling, I'm gonna cover the windows too." He showed on video as the electronic window covers were lowered on both sides of the windows. "That should keep the glass from shattering if there's anything going on."

There was nothing left to do except watch the video screens. All eyes were glued on the screen that followed the green car. It approached the driveway and turned in to everyone's amazement. It entered the long driveway and didn't slow down until it hit the spikes. All four tires popped and the car came to a stop.

Walter yelled, "Get that security team to back off. This smells of a bomb. Everybody get down, that car's gonna blow."

The explosion was massive. The ground shook and everyone felt it. "Everybody okay?" Walter asked as he frantically checked his security screens. "Dang it! The screens are down. The explosion has knocked 'em out. We gotta check on that security team. I don't think they had enough time to get outta the way."

Sam and Brett raced out the back door to have a look only to return a few moments later with frustration written all over their faces. "The team didn't make it out on time. We got casualties."

"Dang it! I shoulda smelled that trouble a lot sooner than I did." Walter shook his fist. "Campbell got me twice now. It won't happen again, you can count on that."

****

Seated in the briefing room, Commander Steele addressed the

group.

"We have learned that the Brothers of Mayhem have been spotted in the area. Alexi, Sergei, and Yuri Deklumkova are very likely seeking revenge for the death of their brother, Dmitri. I want Ruthie and Walter Green to have bodyguards with them at all times. Brett and Sam, don't let them out of your sight."

Sam nodded to Brett. "They'll be well protected, sir."

"We are still searching for signs of any subs in the area. It's not an easy target to conceal so we'll find it eventually. All it takes is one slip on their part."

"What about the surveillance on the green car. Did we get any information from it before it appeared in our front yard and blew up?" Sam asked.

"We did track it to several locations. It went to the marina and Rock Mountain Lookout." Commander Steele passed a few photos to Sam. "They must have had a scrambler system in use because we could not hear any conversations. At some point they must have discovered our tracker and removed it." He stood and walked to the coffee pot. "We believe the car was already rigged with remote control capabilities. This was definitely a message that they know where we are and that they don't like us watching them."

"I'm going to check out Rock Mountain Lookout," Sam said.

"No, you're not." Commander Steele poured coffee into his cup. "I've reassigned you to protecting Ruthie and Walter. I have teams that can investigate Rock Mountain Lookout." Commander Steele returned Sam's glare. "I'm counting on you and Brett to be there for Ruthie and Walter." He sipped his coffee. "When Alexi, Sergei, and Yuri come calling, I want them to meet you two. You are my top pick for that job, Sam. Don't let me down."

****

"Oh stop yer belly achin', Sam. We got work to do. If them Deklumkova fellers want to get at me and Ruthie, they's gonner have to come and get us. An' let me tell you, we ain't gonner make it easy for them. We'll be waiting with some tricks up our sleeves."

"I just don't like the idea of sitting around here when I should be out searching for Carly."

"Aww heck! We all wanna find Carly. They got every possible agent working on the case. They'll find her real soon, don't you worry none. Now, straighten yerself up and let's get to work around this place here." Walter rolled up his sleeves and started barking out orders. "Brett, I need them cameras back up and running so's I can see what's going on around this place."

"Yessir!" Brett set out straight away to get his job done.

"Sam, I need you to come up with a plan for that car training ground. We can lead 'em back there and get them tangled up in our web. They won't stand a chance if we do it right."

Chapter 24

Letter and Pictures

The doorbell rang and Commander Steele stepped inside. He removed his hat and nodded to everyone seated at the kitchen table. Sam, Brett, Walter, and Ruthie were going over plans to trip up the Deklumkova brothers.

"When our team was out searching for clues, they found this letter when they returned to their car." Commander Steele handed a white envelope to Sam. "It's addressed to you, Sam."

"Have a seat, Commander. I'll get you a cup of coffee." Ruthie got up and rummaged around the kitchen to get a coffee for the Commander and a plate of snacks for everyone.

Sam tore the envelope open. He pulled out a letter and three pictures, tossed the letter aside, and looked at the pictures first.

The first picture was of a female. She was tied to a chair with a hood covering her head. Her hands and feet were tied to the chair. A bomb was placed on the floor near her left foot, but it did not appear to be activated. Tools were on the floor beside it, which made Sam believe the installation was in progress.

The second photo showed the woman without the hood. It was Carly. She was wearing a baggy gray track suit. Her right eye was swollen shut, her nose looked busted and she had a fat lip. Sam went cold when he saw that and quietly showed the photo to Brett.

The third photo showed a smiling Monique with arms outstretched, standing on the cliff with the ocean in the background. Her long brown hair pulled into a ponytail. She wore red Capri pants, white boat shirt, and white sneakers.

The letter was short and read:

My Darling Sam,

I have been having the best visit with your wife, Carly. I can see why you dumped me for her. She's so charming. I fixed myself up just for you so that you would like me better. How do you like me with your wife's long brown hair? I borrowed her clothes too. This way you can see that I can be equally as charming.

Once your precious Carly is gone, you will see that you should have stuck with me.

All my love,
Monique
xxoo

"We will get her, Sam. You can count on us. I'll send those pictures and that letter to the lab so they can go over them with a fine-tooth comb. If there are any clues, we'll find them. I'll have teams out there searching day and night. We'll stop at nothing." Commander Steele put the letter, pictures, and envelope into a plastic bag and stood to leave. The room was completely silent when the screen door slammed behind him.

Sam excused himself and went to Carly's room. He sat on the bed and cradled a pillow in his arms. He sniffed her perfume scent and looked around. "Where are you, Carly? If only you could send me a message telepathically." He rocked back and forth hugging the pillow tight.

Chapter 25

Brothers of Mayhem

Alexi was spotted in town getting into a blue pickup truck. He was a very big man sporting huge muscles like he could be a champion weight lifter. His black hair, mustache, and beard made him look like an angry lumberjack.

Sam was making finishing touches to the sea crate when Walter set off the alarm. "Blue pick-up truck's coming in our direction. You ready out there?"

"Just about. I'll need you to keep him busy for a few more minutes. I'll give you the signal when I'm ready."

"You got it!" Walter rubbed his hands together in anticipation of a little bit of fun. "Hey Ruthie, you ready?"

"I'm all tucked inside the sniper tower. Got my six shooter at the ready."

"How about you, Brett?"

"Ready as I'll ever be."

"We're ready to roll. Whatever you do, keep them headsets on so's we can keep in communication with each other. Stay safe out there, and have a little bit of fun."

The blue pick-up truck pulled into the driveway and stopped.

Walter fingers hovered over the control board and waited for just the right moment.

The truck revved its engines three times then drove forward.

Walter raised the wall in front of the house which caused the truck to pick up speed in an effort to beat the wall and ram into the house. Then Walter deployed the spikes and the truck came to a stop.

Alexi got out of the truck and balled his hands into fists. He grabbed his GSh-18 sidearm out of the truck and started walking toward the house.

A cardboard cutout of Ruthie popped up from the ground at the side of the house. Alexi aimed and fired at the cutout making precise hits at Ruthie's cardboard head and heart. He then turned and walked to the opposite side of the house. When he got to the side of the house he found the house wrapped in barbed wire.

"Yoo hoo, I'm over here." Ruthie waved her arm from the sniper tower so Alexi would see her and come in her direction. She ducked back inside. The tower was bullet proof but Ruthie recognized Alexi's Russian military sidearm and knew it was capable of defeating current body armor. Ruthie's next move had to be accurate and swift.

Alexi began running in Ruthie's direction. Ruthie waited patiently until he reached the marked area then she pointed and shot. The dart landed on Alexi's chest and startled him. He looked down at the dart and pulled it out easily.

He shouted up to Ruthie, "You think this will stop Alexi?" He paused to laugh then charged toward the sniper tower.

"You won't be laughing long," Walter said to the screen from inside the house. "That ain't no ordinary dart. It's a wireless taser and you won't like it when I hit this here button in 3, 2, 1, presto bammo."

Alexi stopped running and did a sort of chicken dance as he fell to the ground. He lay on his back and shook occasionally as waves continued to zap through his body.

Ruthie cheered from her tower and thanked Walter for leaning on the button at the right time. "Any longer and he would've been up here. That's one down and two still to go."

Brett and Sam rushed over to keep Alexi under control until the task force arrived to take him away. Meanwhile, Ruthie slowly climbs down from the sniper tower.

"You coming in the house now, Ruthie?" Walter asked.

"Yeah I'm coming. I'm an old lady and it'll take me a while to get there. You better put the kettle on so's I can have a cup of tea when I get there. Better yet, make me a pot of tea so's I can de-stress with a bunch of cups of tea."

"I can do that fer ya. We can play a game of Oklahoma Gin too. That'll take yer mind off things."

"That sounds good. I got the shakes a little bit thinking about the two brothers still to come visit. Next time I'm staying in the house with you where it's comfy. We'll have snacks and make a party out of watching Sam and Brett do all the work. I'm getting too old for this kind of stuff."

"What do you think we should have for supper tonight?"

"I cain't think about supper right now. Let me drink my pot of tea and think on it. I gotta calm my nerves first."

Sam heard the conversation through his headset and offered a suggestion. "I make a pretty good cheese omelet if anyone is interested."

"I like the sound of that," said Walter. "Can we have toast on the side?"

"You bet we can. You and Ruthie just kick back and relax with your tea and game of gin and I'll take care of everything."

Chapter 26

Sergei

Walter welcomed Ruthie in the house with a warm hug and a smooch on the cheek. "I got the pot of tea right here on the coffee table fer ya, Ruthie. You jes come and sit down on the couch and relax. You tell ol' Walter what you need and I'll run and git it fer ya."

"Jes the tea and a chance to sit down on the comfy couch is all I need right now."

Walter sat down beside Ruthie on the couch and dealt the cards. Each player gets ten cards and the rest are turned upside down in the pile with one card turned up. Ruthie's hand had an ace of diamonds, ace of clubs, two of diamonds, three of diamonds, five of hearts, ten of clubs, jack of hearts, queen of clubs, and king of diamonds. She sorted her cards so the ace, two, and three of diamonds were at the right hand side together. She passed on the seven of spades as the first card turned up.

"So's you gotter remember that seven is the maximum number of points you gotter have to knock. Plus it's double points this round."

"Why don't you write that down, Walter? You know I cain't remember that."

"All right, I will. You don't have ta be cranky about it."

After nine turns Ruthie knocked with one point left in her hand. She had ten, jack, queen of clubs; one, two, three of diamonds; three, four, five of hearts. The ace of clubs was her one point leftover. When the hands were tallied, Ruthie had 40 points.

The door opened just then. Sam and Brett walked in. "Alexi won't be a problem anymore. He's in custody."

"Did ya have any trouble with him?" Walter asked.

Brett was the one to give an answer, "Not really. Once the tazer wore off he was a little feisty but they got him into the police car and out of here quick. Now I'm looking forward to watching Sam make omelets. He made me hungry just mentioning it."

Walter and Ruthie continued to play cards while Sam and Brett talked. They moved the cards around in their hand this way and that way. They shifted their heads from one side to the other. They picked up their one card from the deck and threw their one card on top of the deck. Walter knocked with two points left in his hand. The score was now Walter with ten points and Ruthie with forty points.

"Dang it, Walter. I was just about there. Why'd you have ta go an' spoil my fun?"

"Sorry 'bout that. A man's gotta win a round once in a while too ya know."

New cards in hands and tongues out to the side of their mouth, they played the next round while Sam set about to work on the omelets. He tucked a tea towel in his pants to act as an apron. Then he looked through the fridge and pulled out ingredients one by one.

As he washed his hands with soap and water he said over his shoulder, "Brett, you can set the table."

While Sam whisked the eggs in a bowl Ruthie knocked with one point left in her hand. The score was now Walter with ten points and Ruthie with 48 points.

"That sure smells good in there. I'd like a little onion in mine and some green pepper too."

"Your wish is my command, Walter. What do you want in your omelet, Ruthie?"

"I like the sound of what Walter asked fer."

"All right then, two omelets coming up with cheese, onion and green pepper. You two can play one more round of cards and then you better come and sit at the table. You can finish your game later."

"Yessir! Come on Ruthie. I can feel I got a gin in me fer this round."

Ruthie tried not to smile when she looked at the hand she was dealt. Three of spades, three of hearts, three of clubs; six of diamonds, six of clubs; eight of spades, eight of hearts, eight of clubs; jack of spades, jack of hearts. She sorted her hand by placing the trio of three's on the right side of her hand and the three eights beside them. Five turns later she called out, "Gin."

Walter heaved a huge sigh and placed his cards down on the table for counting. Walter's score was still ten while Ruthie's score was 88.

"Aww shucks, Ruthie. It was supposed to be my turn to call gin. After we eat them omelets I bet I'll win a round. Race ya to the table."

Walter stood and pretended to shuffle his feet fast to the table. Ruthie out-shuffled him and got there first. Brett had been put to work slicing oranges. They all gathered at the kitchen table and chowed down on Sam's cooking.

Sam excused himself to sit in Carly's room.

"I don't know why you don't jes sleep in there, Sam," said Ruthie.

"I just like to sit in her room and see if I can imagine where she may be. It helps me think. It's sort of like it's her sanctuary. I prefer to sleep on the couch so I can keep her memory fresh. I bought the new blanket so I could be comfy on the couch. It's no biggy. If

Brett can sleep on the porch every night on sentry duty, I can sleep on the couch as his back-up. This way I know you and Walter are safe. If I hear any noise I'd be up in a flash."

****

"Gin," cried Walter. "It's about time too! I was about to think we was gonna run outta cards and have to deal all over agin. That's ten points fer me an' 88 fer you."

The next hand, Walter knocked with a saucy attitude leaving Ruthie a little stunned. Walter was catching up with 44 points. Ruthie stayed at 88 points.

The alarm sounded and everyone raced to the TV screen to see what was setting it off. They all put on their headsets when they saw it was a white SUV barreling down the highway.

"I'm guessing that's either Sergei or Yuri," said Sam. "Sorry to say this, Ruthie, but we're going to need your help. That SUV won't be going anywhere once it catches up to Alexi's blue truck on the spikes. We'll need him to see you so he runs towards the obstacle course. When we give you the word you can duck into the cellar doors to Headquarters. Once he's clear of the house you can go back to the house and finish your game of gin with Walter." He patted her on the shoulder and said, "Don't worry. Headquarters will be ready to get you out of the danger zone quickly."

"I ain't no sissy. I can do this. Them Deklumkova boys ain't got the best of ol' Ruthie yet!"

"That's my girl," said Walter. "I need you to git back here safe and sound so's I can whoop your sorry butt in gin all fair and square like."

****

Just as Sam predicted the white SUV came to a stop when it hit the spikes behind Alexi's blue pick-up truck. Sergei got out and looked around before looking inside Alexi's truck. He turned when he heard Ruthie's "Yoo hoo, I'm over here."

Right on cue he rushed in Ruthie's direction and pulled out his gun, shooting as he ran. It was dark but he could see her white hair off in the distance and followed. "Here Ruthie, Ruthie. Why don't you let Sergei ketch up with you. We hef things to deescus. Like where's my brother, Alexi, and why you keeled Dmitri. We play leetle shoot 'em up game. Jes me and you. My turn to win."

****

Headquarters was waiting quietly in the basement and the rescue team pulled Ruthie inside the cellar doors to safety. She waited there until she heard back from Brett and Sam on the headsets. "He took the bait. He's following Brett and his lovely white wig. He's far enough away from the house that Ruthie can go back to Walter now."

Walter was waiting upstairs by the open door and pulled Ruthie inside. They bolted the doors and Walter put the security covers over the windows. They could watch the screens and listen to Sam and Brett's progress with Sergei on the obstacle course.

"Not much we need to do except listen, watch and play gin. Those boys have everything all under control out there. Sergei won't be bothering with our Ruthie when they's done with him."

"OK, Walter, but be prepared for me to win."

"I don't think so, my dear. I got that feeling I'm gonna win."

The cards were dealt, they each looked at their cards. Ruthie gave her best glare to Walter and the card playing began. Maximum to knock was five points. Three turns later Walter knocked with two points left in his hand.

"What in tar nations? I just barely got started. You musta fixed that card deck when I was gone out there risking my life away an' all."

"I didn't fix no card deck. This here is what you'd call talented card playin'. You don't stand a chance when ol' Walter's setting across the table from you playin' cards."

"Oh, you are so funny. You only got 51 points. I'm the one with 88 points. I got the lead and I'm gonna finish you off very soon."

While they were bickering they saw on the screen that Sergei tripped the wire and set off the fireworks.

"It's jes like the fourth of July out there. Your turn to deal them cards my dear," said Walter.

They heard gunfire and stopped to watch the screen. Sam was heard saying "We got him. We're going to need an ambulance down here. Put up the lights so the emergency crew can find their way to us. He's a mess. He ran into the tripwire and got the full blast of the punji stake. That bamboo spike went right through his thigh. There's blood everywhere and he's not moving."

****

"The ambulance is gone and Sergei won't be bothering you anymore, Ruthie." Sam said when he and Brett returned to the house. "That's two down and one still to go. I think we should keep the security walls up as a precaution. Yuri still has to make an appearance. We are quite certain he will be showing his ugly face around here next."

"Whatcha got planned fer him, Sam?" Ruthie asked.

"I'm looking forward to taking your car out for a test drive. I'm hoping Yuri will be following me. It'll be fun. So, who's winning the gin game?"
"That'd be me," said Walter. "I only let her have the lead so's to keep her happy."

"You jes deal them cards and we'll see who's winning and who's losing. I ain't finished here yet."

"Awww Ruthie, you gotter let me win. I'm jes a poor ol' defenseless man. You know I need to win so's to keep the peace around here."

"I don't think so. There'd be no living with you if you were to win. I'm gonner win and keep you in line."

After the longest round ever Ruthie cried "Gin! Ha, take that old man."

Walter's jaw dropped when she laid her cards down. Ruthie had ace of spades, ace of clubs, ace of hearts; two of clubs, two of hearts, two of spades, two of diamonds; four of hearts, four of diamonds, four of clubs. Walter's score of 51 didn't hold up to Ruthie's score of 115.

"Dang it! Next time we play gin you better look out. I got a feeling it'll be my turn to win."

They all had a laugh together which helped ease the tension from the day's events.

Chapter 27

Yuri

The next day they waited and watched for any signs of Yuri. The tow trucks had come and gone taking Sergei's white SUV and Alexi's blue pick-up truck with them. The front of the house was back to normal with the spikes back under cover. The only signs of trouble were the walls still firmly in place in front of the house and the barbed wire surrounding the back of the house.

"If Yuri won't come to us, why don't we go out and see if we can find him. Who's up for a drive to town to pick up pizza?" Sam asked.

"I like pizza with just cheese," said Walter. "Just plain fer me. Make sure you get them bread sticks to go with it and soda pop. I like the green soda pop the best. I'll stay here and watch the monitors while yer all gone."

"All right, plain pizza for Walter, the works for me, what kind do you like Brett?"

"I'd like a Hawaiian pizza and some spicy chicken wings."

"Mmm that sounds good, I want some chicken wings too," said Walter.

"You better not get the hot and spicy ones, Walter. It'll give you bad breath and you'll be up all night with heart burn."

"Aww, Ruthie, you're no fun. OK, I'll get the plain chicken wings then. I never liked that ol' heart burn anyhow."

"How about you, Ruthie? What kind of pizza would you like me to order?"

"I like pepperoni pizza. Are we actually gonna get to eat it if we's got Yuri in tow?"

"We'll be eating pizza tonight. Don't you worry. Yuri will follow us home, we'll get Headquarters to send out a team to pull him out of the hole we'll put him in and then we'll come back here to eat pizza with Walter. Just as easy as that."

"OK, Sam, you go ahead and order it and me and Walter'll be waiting for you to come back with it."

"Well, actually, I need you to come along for the ride. Brett too. The three of us have to go. Yuri has to see you in the car or he won't follow us home."

"Can I bring my six shooter and all my favorite guns?"

"You sure can. The more the merrier."

"Hot dang, I'll be ready in a jiffy."

Ruthie disappeared to her room and returned dragging a bag filled with goodies just like Santa Claus.

Brett jumped to help her. "Here let me help you with that. There's a lot of stuff in here. Do you really need it all?"

"It sure can't hurt. I brought all my favorites. I got three bullet proof vests. One for each of us. There's a paintball gun in there, my favorite rifle, my favorite six shooter, there's my favorite pistol and ammunition for the lot."

"Make sure you don't ruin the pizza when you drive around tight corners. There's nothin' worse than pizza stuck to the top of the box. I don't like my soda pop all shook up neither."

"We'll do our best, Walter. Let's all keep our headsets on and keep in constant contact. We don't know when we might engage Yuri Dekumklova."

The drive into town was quiet and uneventful. They parked in front of the pizza restaurant. All three of them went in because they needed Ruthie to be spotted. If Yuri didn't see her himself somebody was sure to let him know she was in town. Sam placed the pizza boxes in the trunk of the car and tied them down so they wouldn't shift on the way back. He placed the pop in the back seat on the floor. He couldn't guarantee it wouldn't roll around but he figured it would roll less on the floor inside the car than in the trunk. They'd just be sure to open the bottles outside in case they fizzed all over and made a mess. Better to get the fizz mess outside than inside.

Sam made a big effort to hold the doors open for Ruthie when they entered and left the restaurant. He made her wait while he put the pizza in the trunk before he went and held the car door open and helped her get inside. Once inside the car, all three put their bullet proof vests on and prepared for the drive home.

Driving slowly, they took the scenic route all over town. Brett noticed the silver hummer following them when they were leaving town. Sam sped up to see if the hummer would try to keep up. Sure enough, it stayed with them. When Sam slowed down they could see the hummer had darkened windows and they could not see inside. They knew Yuri was bald and ugly but they could not see if he was driving.

The hummer sped up and hit their car in the rear knocking them forward. Sam sped up with the hummer in hot pursuit.

"Hey Walter, can you open the gate to the back entrance so we can get to the driving range faster?"

"Sure thing buddy. All it takes is a flick of the switch and it's done."

"Thanks, Walter. Hey can you see this hummer on our tail?"

"Yep, I sure can. Headquarters tells me they spotted Yuri getting into it earlier today. So's you got your man. Stay safe and don't mess up that pizza."

"Don't you worry about the pizza. I secured it in the trunk. It won't be moving no matter what we do. The only thing that'd knock it around is if I roll the car. I'll try not to do that."

"Gall dang you better not roll that car. Ruthie'd have your head. She loves that thing so much that she polishes it by hand."

"Point noted." Sam looked into the back seat and said to Ruthie, "I'll try my best not to scratch up your baby."

"First off," said Ruthie. "You gotter get Yuri off our case. Secondly, if they's any scratches on my car from this high speed chase it'll give me braggin' rights to be proud of. Jes as long as you get Yuri under control and off the streets so's he cain't hurt nobody else."

"That sounds fair enough. No wonder you didn't squawk when he rear ended us back there. Everybody got their seatbelts on? We're about to go joy riding."

They played a game of speed up and slow down to make sure the hummer was seriously trying to come after them. Sam sped up when he came near to the back entrance to the driving range and roared through the gate. The hummer followed at high speed. They raced around the crazy eight patterns then over gravel roads that disintegrated to barren land. They jumped over hills and along bumpy roads that appeared along the course. All the while the tires were squealing and spitting rocks every which way. Now and then Sam would allow Yuri to catch up and side swipe the car. Made him feel like he was gaining on them.

Yuri shot at their tires but Brett was able to reinflate them with his control panel. Ruthi took aim at Yuri's driver side window with the paintball gun and plastered the hummer with several smudges. Yuri made attempts to fire back but Ruthie was able to close her bullet proof window before he could take aim and fire.

"I see it up ahead. The piece de resistance. This is our grand finale, folks. Are you ready, Walter?"

"I'm as ready as I'll ever be. You just be sure to get out of the way quick."

"You're talking to me, Walter. I'm Sam the quick."

"All right then, Sam the quick. Jes be sure an' do yer job properly."

"Roger that. Here we go."

They could see the sea crate ahead of them. There was a ramp leading up to it and Sam headed straight to it with Yuri in hot pursuit. Sam drove up the ramp at high speed and out the other side. Brett pushed the control to set off the rocket launcher and the shiny black charger shot out of the open end of the sea crate and sailed into the horizon landing extremely clear of the sea crate. Sam stopped the car and they all turned to watch out the back window.

Yuri followed them up the ramp into the sea crate and drove out the open end just like they did. He, however, did not have rocket booster capacity and his front end dropped down into the huge hole. They could see the back end of the hummer barely sticking up out of the ground. Then they watched as the special team came out of camouflage and surrounded the hole that Yuri was in.

"Our job is done here. Let's get that pizza back to Walter while it's still hot. I sure hope he doesn't demand his money back if we went over the routine delivery time."

"Oh Sam!" said Ruthie. "He'll be happy just to see us in one piece."

"We may have taken care of the Brothers of Mayhem, but we still have one submarine to deactivate and we also need to find my wife. I sure hope she'll be in one piece when we find her or I promise there will be hell to pay."

Chapter 28

Parcel Delivery

Warning signals went off and everyone in the house ran to the TV to see what the trouble was. The screen lit up and showed a brown papered parcel sitting at the edge of the driveway.

"How in tar nations did they get past our cameras?" Walter scratched his head. "They're playing games with us. Don't nobody go near that parcel. We'll send the bomb squad technicians out there to check it out."

The only people allowed out were the EOD team. They were highly trained in Explosive Ordnance Disposal. The ammunitions technicians were known for taking their time because rushing usually ends in disaster. They stayed behind a protective barrier and sent the RCV out. A remotely controlled vehicle also affectionately named a "wheelbarrow". The technicians wore specialized protective suits that had internal cooling, amplified hearing, and communications back to the control area.

Walter was the man at the communications control with Headquarters backing him up. They could monitor the situation on their screens and see every detail.

The RCV was sent out to the parcel very slowly. It placed a box over the parcel to contain the explosion should the parcel detonate during the process. The box was strong enough to contain the blast. If there was no blast, the box also contained x-ray equipment so they can see inside the parcel to determine if there was in fact an explosive device inside. It could also tell them exactly what type of explosive device they were dealing with.

"Stand down, everyone," Walter announced. "There is no explosive inside the parcel. It is safe to open with care."

To be on the safe side the ammunition tech, wearing the specialized protective suit, opened the parcel and left it for Sam to inspect. The package contained Carly's clothes and the brown wig worn by Monique in the photo. It also contained a photo of Sam and Carly's grandchildren posing with some characters at Disney Land.

"They must be on holiday," Sam said looking at the picture intently. "Commander Steele did mention to me about sending them on a holiday to keep them safe through this entire ordeal."

Commander Steele walked up and put his hand on Sam's shoulder, "Now this is the reason I pulled you off the case. You are too emotionally involved. You let us take care of this one for you, Sam. We'll find Carly and we'll keep your whole family safe."

Sam pursed his lips and nodded. "I know, sir. I just don't like sitting here and doing nothing." He looked at the picture again, "I want to help."
"That is very admirable." Commander Steele patted Sam's shoulder several times. "You did fine work bringing in the Deklumkova brothers alive. They will be very valuable to us once we get them talking." He and Sam walked towards Headquarters keeping pace with each other. "We've been looking closely at that picture of Monique. We think they may be holding Carly near the marina." Commander Steele opened the cellar doors, took one step down then turned and looked back at Sam. "There's been a lot of suspicious activity down there and we'll find out what's going on. We're going to send a team to search every boat." He gave his best supervisory glare to Sam and said, "You hang out with Ruthie and Walter. We'll let you know the minute we find anything." With one final look he said, "You have earned a rest. I expect you to take it." Then he closed the cellar doors behind him leaving Sam standing alone.

****

The desire to search for his wife was too much for Sam. He convinced Brett to accompany him on a little night maneuver.

Ruthie insisted they take along night vision goggles, a thermos of coffee and a container of her brownies. They tried their best to refuse the brownies but they both knew it was a useless effort. Ruthie won the battle due to her long years of mothering her trainees. They knew she was a tough one to argue with once she set her mind to something.

"You make sure you do a thorough search," she said to them. "Don't come back without some solid leads. Goodness knows you two'll git to the bottom of things long before those special teams do." She shook her head and closed her eyes. "They aren't so special, let me tell you. I'd put my money on you two any day over them fellers."

They parked and used the disguise device in the car. "We just have to remember which rock is actually our car when we return. How hard can that be in the dark?" Sam and Brett laughed as they headed toward the lookout. "I still can't believe all the choices we have for disguising that car. It's holographic and it looks so real."

"Yeah," Brett said. "It's pretty cool."

"Are you with us, Walter?"

"I'm right here, Sam. I hear you loud and clear."

"Is Ruthie following along too?"

"Naw, she's in there havin' a bubble bath. She said she gets too worked up worryin' about you. She'll want a full report from me when she gets outta there though. I won't be seeing her for a while, though. She don't come out 'til her fingers go all prune-like."

"I'm standing on the spot that I think Monique was at when that picture was taken." Sam stood and looked in front of him. He could imagine Campbell was standing before him with the camera. "Lord only knows what she and Campbell were thinking at the time. Monique was a pretty twisted creature way back when I knew her." He slowly turned around and looked at all the possible angles that Monique could have looked at that day. "These night vision goggles help me see things around me but it's not quite the same as it would be in the daylight."

"I think I got something over here," Brett said.

Sam made his way over to where Brett was standing near the edge of the cliff. "Well, let's have it. What do you see?"

"There's lights in the distance over the water." He pointed straight out in front of him. "Do you see them? I'd be curious to know what's going on over there."

"That's a lot of bright lights. I say we go and check it out."

Chapter 29

Evening Boat Ride

The classic speed boat was ready and waiting for them at the dock. The grey and silver coloring was just right for them to attempt to sneak in without too much attention. The other boats were loud orange in color and didn't appeal to Sam. He much preferred the classic and admired it for just being a classic. 26 feet, 8 beam with 90 USG fuel capacity. This baby was going to be a treat to drive.

"Why don't you let me drive?" Brett asked with envy.

"No way, I wanna drive her. You can drive on the way back."

"You always do the driving, Sam. It's my turn. Besides, I was the brain child that found the lights."

"All right then. If you put it that way. I owe you one. This time only."

The plan was to drive past the facility and have a look then cut the motor and paddle to shore. They would park the boat someplace quiet and make their way on foot to see what was going on. It was a calm night on the water and they made it to the shore undetected.

They were pleased with themselves for discovering the submarine. They could see it in all its shining glory as they boated by. They were pretty sly to hide it inside a cave. During the day it would be virtually undetectable. Thanks to Brett's keen eyes he found them. Sam and Brett set out to do a little spying and bring back every detail they possibly could. Perhaps they'd even attempt to sabotage the sub before they left if they could get close enough.

They were each clunked on the head from behind and went down like dead weight. When they came to their hands and feet were bound and they were hanging from separate ropes just above water level. Both men had open wounds on their legs that were dripping blood into the water.

"Hello, gentlemen," said Campbell. "Welcome to our little lair." He grinned at them and held his arms up. "What do you think of the place? If we knew you were coming for a visit we would have tidied up a bit more."

"What's this all about, Campbell?"

"Oh, Sam. Tsk, tsk. This is about so many things. Let me think where I should begin." He stood on the edge of the dock looking up at the two men dangling from ropes. "It's simple, really. My darling Monique wanted to see what a nuclear submarine could do so I told her I would show her."

"That is just plain sick," said Brett. "You're willing to put innocent lives at risk just so you can cure your girlfriend's curiosity?"

"Have you ever been in love, Brett?" He put his hand to his chin and said, "Hmm, I remember Carly saying she wanted to fix you up with some of her friends." He nodded his head in a fake sympathetic manner. "I'd say you would like to fall in love some time. It's too bad we have to end your life before that can happen for you."

Sam and Brett looked down to see a shark swimming in the water below them.

"Where is Carly? I demand to see her!"

"Sam, Sam," said Monique as she appeared and walked toward Campbell. "We don't play the game quite that way." She gave Campbell a hug and a kiss on the cheek then turned to face Sam. "I was planning to let you see her but you spoiled all my plans. Now I shall have to punish you for the bad boy you are."

"You have me now so you can let her go."

"Ah, that sounds like such a nice thing to do." She crinkled her nose and twisted her mouth to the side. "But, I don't think so. You see, I'm not really that nice. Sorry about that."

"Why are you doing this to Carly and to us?"

"Well, Sam. If you must know, I will tell you." Monique pulled over a chair and sat down. She had a thoughtful expression on her face. "All those years ago you left me for Carly. You dumped me cold." She shook her head slightly. "I didn't like that too much." She stood and walked a few steps down the dock then turned back to face Sam. "I tried my best to get over you by marrying but I just couldn't find the right guy. They were all so old and died unfortunate deaths." She opened her eyes wide in an exaggerated fashion and put her index finger on her chin. "They were such unfortunate accidental deaths and each one of them left me with bundles of money."

"Yes," Campbell said. "Monique was so grief-stricken when I found her." He put his arm around her and kissed her on the cheek. "I was going through similar difficulties with all my wives. Unfortunate souls that they were, really."

"I was so fortunate to find Campbell when I did. You were only a mere shadow of the man that Campbell is, Sam. I've moved on and you'll just have to accept that I am much happier now."

"If you are so happy then why are you doing this to my wife?"

"You silly dear, Sam. I just needed to let you know that you hurt my feelings." She glared at him. "I don't take kindly to anyone hurting my feelings. I just get rid of them."

"So you see, Sam." Campbell handed a small black device to Monique. "Our little shark friends are hungry. They can smell your blood and can't wait for you to drop in on them for a bite." Campbell laughed. "Our little submarine is all ready to go. Since you were so kind as to bring us this pretty little speed boat we are going to try it out. Once we are far enough away, Monique will push the button on this remote controller and both you and Brett will fall into the water."

"It's pretty simple, Sam. I'll give you plenty of time to say your last prayers before I push the button." She smirked at both men. "It's the least I can do for you." She turned to leave and waved over her shoulder. "Ta ta you two."

The two men watched Monique and Campbell leave in their speed boat. They then focused their attention on the group of sharks swimming in the water below them.

Looking up to see what their rope was attached to, Sam asked, "You got any ideas, Brett?"

"I'm working on a plan but I need a few minutes."

"That's good news. I'll work on the final prayers over here while you work on your escape plan over there."

Chapter 30

Dave Crew to the Rescue

"Any chance we can out swim the sharks when we hit the water?"

"It's doubtful, Sam."

"Have you heard of anyone strong arming a shark and winning?"

"Nope."

"Well I'm willing to give it a try unless you are making headway with that escape plan of yours."

"I almost have these ropes loosened around my wrists. When I get my hands freed, I can try climbing up the rope and get it unhooked. Then I'll come over and cut you loose."

"That sounds good to me. Can you give me a ballpark figure on when you might get that done?"

"Nope. I recommend you try loosening the ropes around your own wrists. It'll help when it comes down to the final seconds of this rescue mission."

"You'd just like to be the one to rescue us, wouldn't you? Well let me tell you, I'm not waiting for you to rescue me. I'll be the one to rescue you."

"You think so, do you? You have to be Sam the hero all the time?"

"As a matter of fact, I do." He pulled one hand free and held it out to show it to Brett. "See, look at this. You're too slow, buddy. I got this thing covered."

"Hardly," replied Brett. "Look at me, I have both hands free."

"Okay, smarty pants. Let's see who can climb up their rope fastest to get unhooked."

"You're on! You're going to owe me big time, Sam the man."

They both reached the top of their ropes at about the same time. Their feet were still bound by rope so they had to use arm strength only. They were madly working on getting themselves unhooked when they heard a motor boat approach. Sam turned to see who was approaching and lost his grip, slipping down the rope.

"Hey you up there! Could you use a little help?"

Sam and Brett were never happier to see the Dave crew in their lives.

"That would be greatly appreciated," Sam answered, clinging to the bottom of his rope. "How exactly are you going to do that?"

"Here, catch." Dave H threw a swiss army knife up and Sam caught it. "See if you can cut the rope with that."

"I'm glad you folded it before you threw it at me."

"Yeah, me too. Sometimes I can be forgetful." Dave chuckled.

"Hey, what about me. You got a swiss army knife for me too?" Brett held his hand out and caught the folded knife.

"You might want to hurry it up. We don't have all night."

"Yeah, Monique and Campbell told us. She's planning on dropping us into the water to be shark food," said Sam.

"It's going to be a pretty big explosion so we really need to get out of here, guys."

Sam cut through his ropes first and dropped down into the motor boat below. Brett was only seconds behind him. They put the boat into high speed and motored out of there as quick as they could.

Dave F pulled out the emergency medical kit and went to work on their leg wounds. "You're lucky. It looks like they only cut enough to draw blood. I'll have this cleaned and wrapped in a jiffy." He looked at their faces and shook his head. "Not too much I can do for the shiners you boys have on your peepers."

"All part of a night's work," Sam said.

When they pulled into the marina Sam asked why they didn't hear an explosion.

"That's because we sort of dismantled their bomb. It wouldn't have been too good to have a bomb going off with a nuclear submarine sitting there."

"How on earth did you manage to do that? How the heck did you even know we were there?"

"Hehe. We snuck in to take a peek at that submarine. Once it was located, the Commander gave us our orders. While you two were dangling there chatting with Monique and Campbell we were busy working."

"Well I for one am glad you were there," said Brett. "I didn't see us getting out of there alive."

"You're welcome, my man." Dave H and Brett high-fived each other. "It's nice to see some appreciation."

"You aren't here for appreciation," Dave N said. "You have some sucking up to do if you want Sam to forgive you for losing Carly in that hotel lobby."

"You lost my wife in a hotel lobby?"

"It was only for a few minutes. Betty was watching her for me. She called me when she walked out of the lobby."

"Is somebody going to fill me in on this story?"

"Oh I can fill you in, Sam." Dave N gave Dave H a sly look and told Sam everything.

"You mean to tell me that you carried my drugged wife off the plane and placed her in a chair in a very public hotel lobby where she slept it off unsupervised?"

"Umm, yeah. Betty was watching her for me."

"You nitwit! Of all the stupid and idiotic things to do. If you were a gentleman you would have put her in a hotel room away from prying eyes. How do you think she felt when she woke up? I trusted you to take care of her for me."

"What do I know about taking care of her? I did my best. Besides, I made up for it by getting her to Ruthie and Walter's place."

"Hey, hey!" Brett stepped between the two men. "So he made a mistake. He admitted he did it. There's nothing we can do to change that now." He turned to Dave H and said, "I think you could give Sam an apology."

"Sorry," he said sheepishly.

"Now it's your turn, Sam. The Dave crew just saved our lives. We were about to be blown to bits and eaten by the sharks. If it weren't for the impeccable timing of the Dave's we wouldn't be here to have this argument. Now shake hands and say thanks."

Sam held his hand out and Dave H grabbed it. They shook three times, a good gripped handshake that both knew had solid meaning behind it. "Thanks for saving my life. I owe you big time."

"No problem, buddy. That's my job." Dave H. patted Sam's shoulder and all was well again between the two. "You should really have a talk with the cab driver that dropped her off in the middle of nowhere in the pouring rain late at night when he was supposed to take her to Ruthie and Walter's place."

Brett stepped in front of Sam and held him back. "Let it go. We have to focus on finding Carly now. Besides, Commander Steele assigned me to look after her. He knew the Dave crew wasn't the best choice for the job. Their specialty is working with electronics and airplanes and stuff like that."

Chapter 31

Some Explaining

Sam and Brett sat quietly in Commander Steele's office. The door was closed but they knew everyone outside, and probably down the street, could hear the yelling they were receiving within.

"I specifically told you to stay put." Commander Steele leaned in nose to nose with Sam. "What part of that order did you not understand?"

"I wanted to help, Grant."

"When you are being dressed down by your commanding officer, you do not call him by his first name." He stood up straight and glared at Sam. "We may be brothers-in-law but right now that doesn't count. I specifically pulled you off this case and you disobeyed me."

"I'm sorry. My wife's missing and in the hands of some real crazy lunatics. I fear for her safety."

"You'll be lucky if I don't send you to the brig for this." He sat behind his desk and looked from Sam to Brett. "What am I going to do with you two?"

"We did find the submarine for you," Sam said.

"Yeah, sure you did. After we already found it ourselves. We sent in the Dave crew to disengage it. You could have ruined everything, not to mention jeopardized their safety."

"If you are going to punish anyone, it should be me. Brett here didn't have anything to do with it. I'm the one that forced him to come along. He was just along to make sure I didn't do anything stupid."

"And how did that go for him?" Commander Steele shook his head and then sighed. "You put me in an awkward position, Sam. I have to place you under house arrest."

"Yes sir." Sam sat quietly looking down at the floor. "I'm thinking about retiring after this mission anyway."

"You don't need to be so hasty about the retirement, Sam. You're a good man and we need you." Grant's demeanor softened. "I'm placing you in the care of Ruthie and Walter. You are not to leave the house for any reason unless I tell you to. Brett will be in charge of making sure you don't get any ideas of leaving the house." Grant pulled out a file from his desk drawer and placed it on the top of his desk. "We are doing everything we can to find Carly for you. We intend to bring her back to you safe and sound. We have a few leads. You have to trust us." Grant opened the door for Sam and Brett to leave. He followed them out. "Join us in the briefing room, gentlemen."

****

Commander Steele silenced the room when he stood. "Dave F, what do you have to report regarding the submarine?"

"Mission accomplished, sir. We dismantled it and tinkered with it a little bit so we now have control of the remote capabilities. That baby's not going to respond to them at all."

"Were you seen by anyone?"

"Not a chance. It was actually a good thing that Sam and Brett were strung up because it kept Monique and Campbell too busy entertaining them to see us. We had plenty of time while they spilled their whole life story."

"Are you absolutely certain you dismantled it?"

"Yes sir, we were very thorough."

"Our men were able to follow Monique and Campbell after they left the submarine lair. They went to another remote island. Our boys will keep a close eye on them in hopes that they lead us to Carly. They are our only hope for finding Carly alive."

"From listening to their dialogue they are two very sick people. They both admitted to marrying dozens of rich spouses and killing them off to get their money," Dave F. reported. "They also sound like they just enjoy setting off bombs for pleasure." He shook his head and said, "and it all seems to come down to the fact that Monique is mad that Sam dumped her to marry Carly all those years ago."

"We're dealing with revenge and insanity. They had impeccable records as our agents up until now. Something made them snap. It's all so unfortunate but I am more concerned for the innocent people they have interfered with." Commander Steele dismissed the meeting and then looked at Sam. "I'll send a medical team upstairs to tend to your wounds. Then I want you to stay put and let us do our job."

"I'll keep a close eye on him for you, Commander," said Brett.

"Good man, Brett. He won't be an easy one to keep down. He's our best agent and I know him well."

"Are you two about done yet?" Sam scowled at them. "I have to get upstairs to watch TV with Walter."

"You better make sure that TV is not the surveillance cameras."

"Of course I mean TV and not surveillance cameras. I'll be good. Scout's honor."

Chapter 32

A Hot Lead

After applying the required stitches, the medics told Sam that he also needed tetanus shot. But instead, they injected a sedative. Anything to keep him from sneaking out again to get into the middle of the action. He passed out cold on the couch where they could keep an eye on him.

Ruthie placed a pillow under his head and covered him with a blanket. "You fellers took a bit of a beating to the face when you was out there gallivanting about." She fluffed a pillow and placed it on her chair then motioned for Brett to sit down. "You set yerself down here and take it easy." He won't be giving you any trouble for a few hours." She pulled the coffee table over. "Here, put yer feet up and get some rest. A bit of shut eye'd do you good right about now. You've been through a lot and need your beauty rest too you know."

"I'll sit and rest a bit. You don't have to worry about me, Ruthie. I'll be fine. You go on back to bed."

"Are you kidding me? I can take a nap later when Walter's watchin' his shows. I wanner stay right here and listen to what you gotta tell me about Monique and Campbell. What do you think's gotten into them crazy fools anyway?"

"They are pretty twisted. I guess some people just can't handle the spy business. It's too much for them and they turn bad."

Walter came shuffling to the living room and sat down in his chair. He was dressed in his usual gray pants, red plaid flannel shirt, suspenders, and navy blue slippers. "Let's see what them special teams is up to." He turned on the TV screen and flicked the switches until he had the surveillance screens up. He turned on the radio so he could hear what Headquarters was talking about. "I wonder if they got any hot leads yet."

"Do you think it's safe? What if Sam hears?"

"Aww he's out cold. Look at him there sleeping like a baby. He won't hear nothin' until at least morning. Besides what other entertainment do you think we's gonna git at this hour in the morning?"

"It doesn't sound like much is going on," said Brett. "You two should go back to bed."

"Nope. We's up now after all that commotion with the medical team fussin' all over you two fellers. No good just lying in bed staring up at the ceiling. I don't know how many times I counted them dead flies up there already. Besides, my bladder was full and I don't know nobody that can sleep through that kinda thing. Once you get up and use the pot then get back to bed," he shook his head. "Sheeesh, then the bed's all gotten cold and it's hard to get comfy again. Old guys like me cain't sleep much no more."

"You can sure sleep through the news!"

"Aw shucks, Ruthie. That ain't sleepin' it's just restin' and takin' all that news in."

"Hogwash to that. You get to snorin' up a storm. Nobody can hear the news once you git to snoring up a storm. Sounds like you's gasping for air before you let out the next snore. Even the curtains is moving in time with your breathin' and snorin'."

"Yeah well I sleep much better in my chair in front of the TV."

"I got an idear," said Ruthie. "Why don't we play a game of crib while we're sitting here doing nothin'."

"We ain't played crib in a long time, Ruthie. I hope I remember how to play it."

"We'll figure it out as we go. I'll go find the crib board. Might take me a bit to find it. Don't you worry none, I'll git it fer us to play."

"I'll put on a pot of coffee while you're looking," Brett said as he made his way to the kitchen.

Walter shuffled into the kitchen to get himself a cup of coffee when Ruthie came in to check the cupboards for the crib board.

"Shhh," Walter put his finger to his lips. "He fell asleep in your chair waiting for the coffee to brew." Walter covered Brett with a blanket while Ruthie propped his feet on a stool. "His so-called tetanus shot took a lot longer to take effect than Sam's did." Walter chuckled softly as he sat down again. "Them medics were perty sly to tell them the sedative was a tetanus shot. Not too many folks can put one past these two. Don't disturb them. They could use some sleep after the rough night they had."

"It's a good thing, too. I cain't find that crib board no matter where I look." She poured a cup of coffee for herself and for Walter. She placed the coffee cups on the kitchen table and looked at Walter. "You and me can play gin here in the kitchen. That way we don't have to watch them two sleep."

"I don't know where the cards went to," said Walter. He knew darn well where the cards were because he was the one that hid them. "That's too bad if we cain't play cards right now." He took the last sip of his coffee and stood. "I think I'll go down to Headquarters and see what's going on. See if they's got any new leads. You stay here and watch them two sleep."

****

"Everything all right upstairs?" General Steele asked as he held his office door open for Walter to enter.

"Yep. Them two are sleeping like babies. Tetanus shot my eye. Neither one of 'em caught on." Walter slapped his thigh and chuckled. "I saw that one comin' a mile away and I'm amazed that

Sam fell for it. He's usually a lot brighter than that!"

"I have a job for you, Walter. That is if you're up to it."

"What kinda job? You know I'm good fer any job you need me fer."

"We're getting ready to send out a team to investigate a lead we have. We think we know where they are holding Carly."

"You definitely got my interest."

"I want you to stay in the van with all the electronic equipment and monitor the situation. The team lead will wear a headset and keep in communication with you the whole time. They'll also need someone to talk them through any situation if they find explosives. We know these two double agents love their explosives so we're ready for pretty much anything at this point."

"You got that right."

"So are you up for the job?"

"Yes sir. I'm in. Jes tell me where to go and I'll be there."

Chapter 33

To The Yacht

Walter was in the surveillance van parked on the street near the marina. There was a driver with him that could also act as an assistant with the equipment. He had direct contact with the team lead in charge of the field mission by way of headsets. The van was equipped with coffee, sandwiches and snacks to last through the night. They were settled in to wait this thing out and hopefully get the results they were hoping for. The desired result was to find Carly Davenport and rescue her alive and well.

Walter was fond of Carly and wanted to do everything he could to rescue her from those crazy agents. He couldn't kick himself hard enough for letting her slip away from him and Ruthie. He prided himself on getting good gut instincts about situations. This time he hadn't felt that gut instinct. He guessed that was because Monique and Campbell knew the inside workings of this mission. They were crafty and had used every trick in the book to sneak in there and take what they wanted.

It was Walter's own personal mission to right the wrong that had happened on his watch. He knew his age and health were not working in his favor, but he was certainly glad he could contribute with his expertise on surveillance equipment and bombs. Nobody had more knowledge of those areas. He had trained all the agents from day one and he continued to work with them in a supervisory role.

"The yacht pulled in a few hours ago and docked at the marina," said Team Lead Oliver. "We can't tell who exactly is on board but there is lots of activity and it appears they are guarding something. I have men in the water and men on shore. The minute we catch sight of Mrs. Davenport in there we are going in."

"Can you git any bugs onto the boat so's we can hear what they're saying?" Walter scanned all the electronic equipment in the van as he spoke. "I'm gonner zoom a camera in on the cabin door so's I can see inside when they open it."

"My men placed several bugs on the hull of the boat. They should give you good reception any minute now."

"That's good. Yep, I can hear some movement. They's not sayin' much but somethin's goin' on. As soon as I get something for you I'll let you know."

"Okay. Roger that."

Walter was munching on a sandwich when he noticed activity. He heard movement first then saw through the video screen that people were leaving the yacht. "Team Lead Oliver, are you there?"

"Yes, go ahead, Walter. I'm here."

"It looks like everyone is leaving the yacht."

"I'm going to send up a scout to have a look around. This could be our chance to get in there."

"Okay. Roger that. I'll keep my ears and eyes open to cover you."

Walter could see smoke coming from the yacht. "Team Lead, is everything okay? I see smoke coming from the boat."

"Yeah, we're fine. They let off some smoke bombs. Nothing serious."

Next Walter saw fireworks going off from the roof of the yacht. "Is somebody having a party over there? What's with all the fireworks?"

"We're not sure, but I think they set them off by remote control. Somebody's sending us a message."

"You fellers be careful. These guys are capable of a lot of mayhem."

"We searched the entire yacht and there's no sign of Mrs. Davenport. They've been playing us to keep us off the trail. We found a note."

****

Ruthie was fussing over Sam and Brett at the kitchen table when Walter walked in with Commander Steele.

"Good mornin', fellers," Walter said.

"Where the heck you been all night? I been worried sick about you thinking you wandered off in the night and was lying dead in a ditch somewhere's getting eaten by the coyotes." Ruthie hugged Walter something fierce and then stood back to smack him in the arm.

"Oww, what'd ya punch me fer?" He held his bruised shoulder to ease the sting.

"That's fer scaring me. You jes wait 'til you do something real bad. That punch'll hurt ten times worse. You coulda tol' me you was gonna be out all night or somethin'."

"I was on top secret business. I couldn't tell you nothin' an' you know that, Ruthie. This spy business ain't new to you."

"Yeah, well, you coulda' sent someone to tell me not to worry 'bout yew." She busied herself at the counter then turned to ask, "Do you fellers want some coffee? I'm makin' bacon and eggs for these two. Won't take much to make more fer you two too."

"Sounds good to me, Ruthie," Commander Steele said as he sat down at the kitchen table. "We have some time to eat while we discuss a few things."

"Walter, since I'm mad at you, I expect you to make toast for everyone. You can set yerself down at the table and make it there."

"Yes, Ruthie. I can make toast. Can I have my egg easy over? Two of 'em if you got enough eggs. I been drinking coffee and eatin' sandwiches all night in that van. Eggs sure sound good, though. You're the best, honey!"

Ruthie set up the toaster on the table in front of Walter. She placed two loaves of bread down. "Make sure you ask if they want white or brown toast. Nothin' worse than getting the toast you don't like." She put a hand on Sam's shoulder and the other hand on Brett's shoulder. "These two are getting special treatment this mornin'. You take care of them first."

"I can make omelets, Ruthie," said Sam. "Let me help you."

"Oh no you don't, young man!" She turned around from the counter and pointed a spatula at Sam. "I'm in charge of this breakfast. You just set yerself down there and enjoy being taken care of. You had a rough night and I'm gonner get you feeling better and back on yer feet." She paused for a moment then turned and asked, "anyone want an omelet? I make a pretty good omelet too, ya know."

Nobody wanted an omelet. They all opted to have easy over eggs so they could sop the yolk up with their toast. All Ruthie heard through breakfast was eager grunts and satisfied groans as everyone dug into their food.

"That was a good breakfast, Ruthie. Thank you for including me. I'll help you with the washing up after we have our meeting." General Steele pulled an envelope out of his coat pocket and handed it to Sam. "This is addressed to you. They found it on Monique and Campbell's yacht."

Chapter 34

Note From Monique

"The team found this letter on Monique and Campbell's yacht. We had the place staked out because we thought Carly was being held on board." Grant Steele stood and took his plate to the sink. "It turned out to be a false alarm. There was no sign of her there."

"They was playin' with us," said Walter. "They set off smoke bombs and fireworks. Thankfully nobody got hurt."

"Is it safe to open this letter?" Sam asked as he turned the white envelope over in his hands. "You're sure it's not booby trapped?"

"Yeah, we checked it over pretty good." Walter nodded his head. "You can go ahead and open it."

Dear Sam,

Isn't it wonderful that you managed to be rescued from my sharks? Next time we meet you won't be as lucky to survive.

I have so enjoyed my little visit with your wife, Carly. She's such a darling little creature. I tried my best to teach her how to box with me but she just couldn't get the hang of it. It's a pity that she bruises and breaks so easily.

My one wish is that you would meet me at our old dream house. We talked about Stone House together as the place we could settle down in some day when we found our fortune.

Well, my dear Sam. I have more than enough money in my bank accounts and bought the place several months ago. I share it with Campbell now.

*It could have been good for you and me but those days are over.
Campbell suits my needs far more than you ever could. You'll
have to move on with your life and forget me. It's better this way.*

*Please do come over for a visit. We have so much to catch up on
with old times and all.*

Much love,

Monique

xx oo

"Are you going to allow me to attend a meeting with Monique,
Grant? Considering I am under house arrest."

"Of course you'll be going. We'll have you wired so we can
monitor your every word and move. You'll wear a bullet proof
vest too." Grant pointed to Walter, "get on the horn and get a team
together. I want the place surrounded with snipers and dogs and
the whole shebang."

Walter headed over to his 80 inch TV that Carly gave him. It was
now his own little control centre. He patted the TV and said,
"We're coming for you Carly. We're gonna bring you back safe.
Hold tight until we can git to you. Save a big ol' hug fer yer old
pal Walter."

"What can you tell us about the Stone House, Sam?"

"Place is like a fortress. It's all made of stone with lots of rooms
beneath ground. There's a massively huge wine cellar down there.
If Carly's down there we got our work cut out for us. There won't
be any communication down there because the stone and rock will
cut everything off."

"I'll need you to draw up a map of the house if you can so the
teams will know what they are getting into. They'll need to know
about all entrances and exits."

Sam sat down with paper and pen to mark down everything he could remember about the place. "It was over 30 years ago so I'm going on memory here. We had a tour when they had an open house but not all areas of the house were available for the general public."

"Walter, see if you can get hold of a real estate company that may know that house. We need every detail we can get. We don't want any surprises once Sam gets in there."

"I'm on it, Commander."

"We're going to need a medical crew standing by too. It sounds like Carly has some intensive injuries. There's no telling what that crazy woman has done to her."

"Right, I'll do that."

"Sir," said Ruthie. "Can I git in on this as a sniper? I'm a dang good shot. I never miss my targets. You just put me in a location with a good view and I'll be no trouble to anyone."

"I don't want you on your own so I'll make sure the team lead places you with a partner. You gotta promise me you won't be trying any heroics out there."

"I promise to behave myself, Commander. I want to see Carly git out of there safe and sound."

"All right. You're on. Welcome aboard. Go and get yourself kitted out down in Headquarters with the rest of the outfit."

"Thank you, sir! You won't be sorry you put ol' Ruthie on the job." She danced around in circles then went over and kissed Walter on the cheek before she went out the door to get ready with the team.

Chapter 35

Sam Remembers

A little solitude was needed before Sam went out to meet with Monique so he decided to take a much needed shower. It wasn't all that long ago that he had a steamy shower with Carly. Although she didn't know it at the time that was supposed to be a last love session before Sam went into danger. Little did he know he would be remembering that shower when Carly was the one missing and needing to be rescued.

He looked at his naked form in the mirror. Carly always said he was a good looking man. Maybe she just said that to puff up his aging ego. As he looked himself over in the mirror he thought maybe he was in pretty good shape. He put his fingers to his eyes to stop the flow of tears. He was determined not to cry but he just didn't know how to handle his emotions. Carly meant everything to him. He never thought for one moment that she would ever be placed in danger. Of all the stupid and idiotic things he wondered why he ever lied and said he bought an airplane. Only his sweet and lovely Carly would believe a fool story like that. She had faith in him and he blew it big time by lying to her like that.

If only he could go back in time and make a change of plans so that Carly wouldn't have been put in the line of danger. He kept racking his brain to think of how he could have done things differently. He wondered why it was that the enemy liked to go after family members. It's not their fault and they have no way to protect themselves for such attacks.

Sam stepped into the shower and stood under the hot water. He bent his head foreword to soak his head. He closed his eyes and felt the heat waking up his body after the effects of the sedative the night before. He woke up feeling sluggish but after reading that letter from Monique he had a surge of adrenaline through his body. He was alert and ready to go in. They say hell hath no fury like a woman scorned but he saw it differently in this situation. Monique never had a stronghold on his affections, ever. He didn't know who she thought she was to do all of this. She had no class the way Carly did. Monique couldn't hold a candle to Carly. She was just plain crazy to think up this ridiculous scheme of revenge. She was getting on Sam's last nerve and she better be ready for his wrath.

Monique had been his trainee and he was just doing his job. He taught her everything he could and she caught on well. She had some skills and put them to work on the job. She was very competent in self defense and didn't need much help there. She could handle herself in a fight. He thought of her as one of the guys he worked with and nothing more. They had one fling and he couldn't even remember much about it. It was a mistake and he thought they'd both agreed at the time that it was a mistake and should never be repeated. They had a duty to their work first and emotions would just get in the way.

He cringed to think of the damage Monique could have inflicted on Carly. He couldn't think why anyone in their right mind would hurt her. Then again, Sam knew that Monique was not in her right mind. She was twisted and bitter and crazy. If she killed all her ex husbands as easily as she said she did then there was a fine line to work with to get Carly out of there safely. Sam would take great pleasure in wrapping his hands around Monique's throat. It was Sam's intention to make sure Monique didn't make it to jail. He wanted blood and would settle for nothing less. Campbell's blood too. Heads were going to roll and today was the day for it to happen.

Finished his shower, he wrapped a towel around his waist and padded his way to Carly's room. He closed the door behind him. He hadn't allowed himself to spend much time in her room for fear he would get too emotional. Now it served to motivate him for the task at hand. He could smell her in this room and she was in his head. Her presence strengthened him and gave him the power to do what had to be done.

He sat on the bed. She probably chose a pink and white bed covering to get back at him. If she was mad about all the troubles she had after the plane landed on Summerview Island, this would be her way of fighting back. She knows pink isn't his favorite color. He always gave her a hard time about the color scheme of their bedroom at home. It had to be blue because that was his favorite color. A man couldn't survive in a pink master bedroom. He was pleased that she always compromised and said she understood. She worked with many shades of blue throughout their 30 years of marriage.

Carly was a gifted quilter and he was proud of the work she did. Every room in their home had homemade quilts for the beds. She even had spares in the linen closet. She always got compliments from overnight guests. She even gave quilts to some of his work mates when an occasion came up such as birthdays or Christmas gifts. If she wasn't quilting she was baking. He was always carting food to work to share with the guys. There were never any crumbs left over after the guys got a hold of it.

Sam saw the clothes hanging in the closet for the grandkids. An airplane sleeper for baby Cooper. She was never going to let him live it down that he lied to her about buying an airplane. He couldn't even afford a paper airplane let alone a private jet.

He wasn't normally a praying man but if anyone was listening up there he was willing to talk. He'd give anything to get Carly back in his arms safe and sound. To see her smile in the way that he knew it was only a smile for him. He promised to do things for her around the house and to take her out on the town once in a while. She always looked great when she got all dressed up and put on makeup and jewelry. He would buy her the biggest diamond ring for her finger that he could afford and take her out for dinner. If that was what it would take to get her home safely, Sam was willing to ask for it in a prayer. Carly was the only one for him and he couldn't manage without her in his life. They'd made it through thirty years of marriage and he wanted to get through another thirty years to come.

Commander Steele pounded on the bedroom door bringing Sam back to reality. "Hey princess, are you about ready in there? Don't forget to put on your makeup and bring your purse!"

"Hardee har har," Sam hollered back. "I'm on my way out." He quickly put on his clothes and took one last sentimental look around the room. He didn't intend to return until this mission was resolved.

Chapter 36

Meeting Monique

The sign out front said "Welcome to the home of Monique and Campbell." Sam thought that was a lot of bull. There's no welcome feeling in this place. The coldness seeps through every nook and cranny. He walked cautiously along the long winding pathway to the front door, always on the lookout for booby traps and trip wires. He rang the doorbell and noted the echo it made.

Monique opened the door and greeted Sam with a hug and kiss on each cheek. "Darling," she said. "Come in. I am so glad to finally have you come for a visit. I've wanted to show off the place to you for a long time now."

"Cut the crap, Monique. I'm not here for a social visit. Where's my wife?"

"Oh but you are here for a social visit, Sam. I won't hear of anything else. Once I get my nice visit then I'll tell you all about Carly." She closed the door behind them and grabbed Sam by the arm pulling him inside the foyer. "Just look at this place. Isn't it lovely?" She walked him down the long hallway into the great room.

It featured three full length floor to ceiling windows on the far wall that had three more full length windows on top of them. The cleaner would have to use a very tall ladder to reach the top of those babies. It gave a grand cathedral look. On either side of the windows were floor to ceiling stone fireplaces. Sam could stand up straight inside the fireplace without hitting his head. Above one fireplace was a moose head and above the other fireplace was a bison head. He wondered if she'd prefer to have his head up there instead. There were two four-seater couches facing one another with a coffee table in the middle. There were two massive matching wing chairs placed together at each end of the couches.

The incredibly high ceiling boasted a huge crystal chandelier. Again, Sam wondered who the poor sucker was that had to clean all this stuff.

"I'll give you the grand tour starting in the great room. We have only one room above ground and that's the tower room. I'll show you that later. Come downstairs and see the wine cellar. I am most proud of that room. We can have wine tasting parties down there. It's my favorite part of this w hole house."

"If I look at your wine cellar will you then tell me where you're hiding my wife?"

"Oh Sam, don't be such a spoil sport. Don't you remember when we came on a tour of this place all those years ago? We held hands and shared our hopes for the future."

"To be honest with you, I don't remember much about it at all."

"Oh come on, make an old girl happy. Just play along and pretend you remember. If you don't I'll have to punish you."

"How much more do you think you can punish me? You already have my wife somewhere and I want her back!"

"You always did say the sweetest things, Sam. I'm going to ignore your persistent questions about Carly. She's fine. I want to spend time with you and forget about everything else. That's all I've wanted all these years you know. Just to have you to myself for an hour isn't too much to ask is it? Now you sit down at this table while I get us a bottle of wine."

"I don't want any wine, Monique. Is she here in this house?"

"You really are getting tiresome with all this talk, Sam. Try to talk about something more interesting." She brought out a bottle of Chardonnay and two wine glasses. "Here we go. Can you open the bottle for us? It's just one little thing you can do for me today. Humor me and play along for just a little bit. It would make me so very happy, Sam."

"I don't want any wine and I'm not going to open the stupid bottle." He threw the bottle down and it smashed on the stone floor. "Now you tell me where my wife is or I'm going to search every room in this house until I find her."

"You silly man, that is exactly what I want us to do. We can tour every room in this house together. We'll talk and laugh together just like old times."

"That's not what I mean." He clamped his hands around her throat and squeezed. "Now tell me where my wife is before I get angry."

Monique's hands flailed and her face turned red as she tried to break free of Sam's grip. He let go to listen to what she had to say.

"Campbell is with Carly right now," she said gasping for air. "He's putting together final touches, if you know what I mean." She grinned, "If he doesn't hear from me in fifteen minutes from now he's going to set off the nuclear submarine."

"Well that won't be a loss," Sam sneered back at her, "The Dave crew dismantled your submarine and they now have control of it." Sam grabbed Monique's throat again. "You tell me where she is. Tell me right now!" He let go of her neck so she could answer.

"All right, all right." She gasped for air and rubbed her hands on her neck. "We'll have to go outside to get there."

"You better not be pulling my leg. I'm not playing your stupid games anymore."

Monique led the way upstairs and out the back door. "Don't you think we have the best view out here? During the daytime it's lovely. Just ocean as far as the eye can see. I'm surprised it took you so long to figure out the ocean clues I sent you." She continued to lead Sam to the cliff edge, then stopped and turned to face him. "If I can't have you I'm going to throw myself off this cliff, Sam. Then you'll never find your precious Carly. Why couldn't you have loved me just a little bit?"

"I never loved you at all, Monique. It was a just a fling between you and me. It was a mistake too, and we talked about that at the time. Why are you being so silly about this?"

"I was in love with you, Sam. I still am in love with you." She walked to the very edge of the cliff and looked over.

Sam made a dash to catch her before she jumped and caught her just in time. "Not so fast. You have to tell me where my wife is."

Monique wrapped her arms around Sam in a hug and felt his gun tucked into the back of his jeans. She pulled it out and backed away with the gun pointing at Sam. "You silly man. I never intended to jump off the cliff. I knew you would try to stop me. You're such a gentleman. It really is one of your biggest faults, you know. You should learn to see through people's facades." She gestured with her head and gun for Sam to move towards the cliff. "I want you to jump, Sam. We could have had a nice visit before it came to this but you couldn't play nice."

"I'm only here to find my wife and you aren't going to stop me. We have people all over this place and you won't get away with this."

She grabbed him from behind and held the gun to his head. "We'll walk nice and slow back to the house. Any sudden moves and I'll shoot your pretty little brains out. Maybe if you're a good boy I'll let you see your wife before I kill you."

Sam flipped Monique over his shoulder and the gun went flying out of her hands. She dove towards Sam's feet and he landed flat on his face. Monique jumped on his back and pinned him down. He rolled over and tossed her across the yard. She stretched her fingers out to reach the gun. They both grabbed the gun at the same time and struggled at the edge of the cliff. Monique kicked Sam down, raised the gun and aimed at his head. Sam closed his eyes and waited. He heard a gun shot but didn't feel anything. When he opened his eyes, Monique stood there with a strange look on her face.

"I've been shot, Sam. This is what you wanted all along, isn't it? I've always loved you." She raised the gun again to shoot Sam when a second bullet got her and she tumbled backwards over the cliff to the rocky shore below.

Looking over the edge, Sam could see her lying on a rock below. She did not survive the bullets or the fall. Sam shook his head and turned to see the Team Lead walking toward him.

"Campbell has Carly somewhere in that house. We have to hurry and find her."

Chapter 37

Searching the Stone House

"Where are we heading to, Sam?" asked the Team Lead. "You point the way and we'll go."

"I think she's in the tower room. Apparently Campbell is with her doing final touches. We need to get to Carly before Campbell finishes whatever he is doing. I fear the worst knowing those two. Their plans are pretty twisted to say the least. We can expect a bomb to be rigged up since we know Campbell gets a kick out of that sort of thing."

"Right, you lead the way. We're right behind you."

They managed to avoid the first trip wire. "The place is booby trapped. Tell your men to be careful."

The lights went out and they stopped to let their eyes adjust. "We got guys with night vision goggles. We'll wait right here for them to come in and lead the way." The Team Lead made the request on his radio and they waited patiently for them to arrive.

"Sam old man. You're too funny." Campbell called out. "Well, you're funny in a pathetic sort of way. You'll never make it to your wife. I have her connected to a bomb and I have the remote control right here in my hand. I'm enjoying this show so much that I'll let you get close enough before I blow you all to kingdom come. You're just an old man now, Sam. Monique has me now and she knows what a real man is like. You're part of the past and about to become history for good this time. You may have gotten away lucky last time but you won't now. I'll dance on your grave."

"Didn't you hear, Campbell?" Sam said. "Monique is no more. She fell for me. Quite literally, she fell off the cliff to the rock below." Sam turned in the direction he thought Campbell was in. "If I have my way, you'll be joining her. I'm here to take you down tonight, Campbell. It's only a matter of time."

"You're telling naughty stories. I don't believe you. Monique and I plan to take a long vacation once this is all over with. We might even take your ashes with us to be scattered at sea. This night belongs to me and Monique."

"No, it's true. Monique is dead. You may as well accept it and turn yourself in now. The game is over. You lost and we won."

"Never! You'll never win, Sam. You'll never see Carly alive again."

They heard footsteps and the sound of a door close. The men with the night vision goggles reported that Campbell disappeared and they couldn't see him anymore. Smoke bombs went off just then and they all scrambled to put on gas masks. One of the men handed a mask to Sam and he put his on as well. They continued on in the direction of the stairs that lead up to the tower room.

"Carly, are you up there?" Sam yelled out but they heard no answer. "Carly where are you? We're here to rescue you and get you out of here safely. Make any kind of noise if you can hear me. It's me, Sam. We're here to rescue you but we can't do this if you don't help us out a little bit."

"We'll have to keep going up the stairs," said the team leader. "If she's there we'll find her. She may be incapacitated and can't hear us let alone answer."

They climbed the winding staircase up towards the tower room. A dog began barking and they continued with caution. They could see the golden lab dog at the top of the stairs. He was behind a baby gate and stood up when he saw the team climbing the stairs. He stood on his hind legs and put his front paws over the gate and wagged his tail. They could see the dog was tied to a chair and in that chair was Carly. Her hands and legs were bound and there was a gag over her mouth. She was unconscious.

They heard Campbell's voice on a speaker in the room. "Take one more step and the gate will open allowing the dog to charge down the stairs toward you. You'll notice he's attached to the chair Carly is in so he'll drag her down the stairs behind him. Then when Carly's chair is pulled it will set off the bomb that is on the table." He chuckled and continued, "I get so much better at these bombs all the time. Nobody has the smarts like I do. My bombs are unique and pretty. Old Walter may have gotten me started with my love of bombs but I have perfected the art. That old fuddy duddy is laughable. He thinks he's able to go toe to toe with me. He's pathetic and old and useless. I'm the King bomb maker now! You have exactly five minutes before I push the button and then you'll all be blown to smithereens. It's been nice knowing you. Bye!"

****

Brett was outside when Campbell came through the door. "We meet again, old buddy," Brett said to him.

"Get out of my way or I'll push the button on this remote and blow the whole place up." He waved the remote so Brett could see it. "They're all in there and they'll all be blown to bits." Campbell smirked and walked away.

Brett ran up behind Campbell and gave him a shove knocking the remote to the ground. Campbell turned around to face Brett. Brett took on an upright stance with his legs shoulder-width apart, rear foot a half-step behind the front foot. "Let's go toe to toe, you and me."

"Don't be silly. You can't take me. I'm better at everything than you are."

Campbell took the first jab at Brett and got him square in the nose. Brett responded by slipping down and throwing several punches to Campbell's stomach. Campbell rammed into Brett knocking him to the ground. He sat on Brett and put his hands around his throat and squeezed in an effort to strangle him. Brett pushed Campbell off him and got to his feet. Campbell tried to get to the remote control but Brett pounded on him and stopped him. Campbell managed to pull a knife out and swung it wildly at Brett.

"Give up now and make this easy on yourself, Campbell."

"Never! I'm a rich man and should be treated with respect."

"You're a menace to society and you'll spend the rest of your days rotting in jail."

Brett wrestled the knife out of Campbell's hand and tossed it to the ground. He then held him down firmly and delivered several punches to Campbell's face. "That's for the way you treated Carly." More intense punches made Campbell's face a bloody mess. "That's for the way you disrespected Walter."

Brett left Campbell mangled on the ground and went to retrieve the remote control. Campbell got up and charged at Brett from behind, knocking him over. Campbell stood up, pulled out a gun, and pointed it at Brett. "This is for what you all did to Monique." He stretched his arm out and prepared to fire when a shot rang out and Campbell fell to his knees. He wavered for a moment and then fell to the ground dead.

Brett said a silent prayer and thanked Ruthie for being such a good shot. He knew she would not have let anyone else take that shot. He held up the remote control and yelled, "I got it. The bomb won't be exploding now." Then he lay on the ground. His injuries were catching up to him. He knew he had a broken nose and possibly a couple of broken ribs.

Chapter 38

Saving Carly

"A sniper just shot Campbell dead," the team lead announced. "Brett's down and the medical team is working on him now. There was a big battle between Brett and Campbell and in the end he kept the remote control away from Campbell so we shouldn't have any surprise detonations while we're here."

"We need to be careful," said Sam. "He's probably got this place wired with booby traps."

The team lead walked up to the next step and they heard a click. "I think I have stepped on a trigger."

"Don't move, stay very still." Sam held his hands up cautioning the guy to stay where he was. Then he hollered at the top of his lungs, "We need some EOD people in here now! Don't anybody make any sudden moves. This place is rigged."

The dog began to jump at the gate and whine. Sam tried to talk to the dog to calm him down while they waited for help to arrive. "It's okay, boy. Everything's going to be okay. Can you sit?" The dog sat down. "Good boy! Now you stay where you are. Stay boy. You sit nice and guard Carly. She needs you right now." Sam pointed to Carly and the dog looked in her direction. He lay down at her feet and groaned as he rested his head on his paws.

"It sure would help if we could see. It's awfully dark in here. Anybody got a flashlight or something?" Sam asked.

"They're going to bring in some portable lights. They don't want to turn on the electricity just yet in case it's rigged to set off explosives."

"Okay, thanks," said Sam. He turned to the team lead and asked,

"How are you holding out? What's your name? It's Ray isn't it."
Sam used his calm voice to talk to the man. "Everything's going to
be all right. We're going to get you out of this, Ray. Just stay as
calm as you can and don't make any sudden moves."

Sweat was pouring down Ray's face. He nodded in response to
Sam. "I have a wife and new baby," he whispered. "Make sure you
tell them I love them."

"Now don't go talking like that. You're going to walk out of here
tonight and you're going to go straight home to that wife and baby.
Do you hear me?"

"My wife's name is Angie." He looked at Sam intently. "I want you
to tell her I'm sorry if I don't make it out of here alive. The baby's
name is Oliver. He's six weeks old." Ray gulped and tried to talk
calmly. "I have all the important papers in the safety deposit box at
the bank. Tell Angie she'll be well taken care of. I did everything I
could to set her up real good in case I didn't survive the job."

Sam was relieved to see the EOD team arrive. The Dave crew was
there as well. Two ammunition techs were dressed in the
specialized protective suits. They put a protective shield around
Ray and looked closely at what his foot had triggered.

In a voice muffled by his protective head gear, the technician told
Ray to remain still. It was important to do these things slowly and
carefully. Any mistakes could end in disaster for everyone on
scene. If Ray could work with them and stay calm, they'd get him
out as soon as they could.

Ray promised to cooperate as best he could.

The Dave team had a toy size remote control helicopter that had
cameras attached. They sent it up to the tower room so they could
scan the area and assess the traps that were set out for them. They
could watch the pictures from the laptop computer.

"There are several bomb devices in the room." Dave H announced.

"It looks like they are weight activated. Carly isn't on one but the dog is. We need to keep the dog very still. We need someone to use a tranquilizer dart on the dog to keep him from moving while we work."

"Someone get a tranquilizer gun," Sam yelled. "Make it quick, we need to calm this dog down as soon as possible."

Sam was lost in thought as he watched Carly sleeping in the chair. He felt helpless to protect her. She was in need of medical attention and he wished he could whisk her away immediately. He could picture her looking up at him on their wedding day when she agreed to be his lawfully wedded wife. He could picture her holding their first child with the look of pride and exhaustion at the same time. Mostly, he didn't want to lose her. Not this way. Not any way. He would never allow her to be in danger again if the good Lord would just let them get out of this mess they were in.

"Sam," the muffled voice of the suited EOD technician brought Sam out of his day dream. "We're going to cover you with a shield as well. It's better if you can stay here and talk to Ray. He's looking like he might give in to panic. Keep him calm. Can you do that for us?"

"Yes, I can do that. Ray, it's me and you here, buddy. You gotta talk to me. Tell me about that baby of yours. It's Oliver, right?"

"We didn't think we could have kids, Sam. Poor Angie had so many miscarriages. We pretty much gave up. Then she noticed she was gaining weight." Ray chuckled and shook his head. "She kept asking me if I thought her butt looked fat. You know a woman, that's the worst question a man could walk into." He laughed and continued. "She finally went to the doctor and we were both shocked when she was told she was pregnant." He shook his head. "It was like a miracle and we were ecstatic. Angie went shopping immediately she was so happy. She had the baby's room all ready before she was even six months pregnant."

"Excuse me, gentleman." A sniper stood beside Sam. "I'm going to need you to lean over a bit so I can get a good aim at the dog with this tranquilizer gun." He leaned past Sam, aimed and shot. "That'll do. Thanks guys." He turned and walked back down the stairs.

Sam watched the sniper leave and wished that could be Ray walking out of here safely. "Don't let anything happen to that dog. He's a nice dog and this isn't his fault."

"We'll do what we can, Sam." The EOD gently placed a protective cover over the sleeping dog and said, "No promises, but we'll try."

"Yeah, well if you can save him through all this I think I might want to take him home with me. He's a beautiful dog."

"After making the initial assessments," the suited EOD tech said. "We're going to set up an electronic buzz to keep all electronic devices frozen. We want to get Carly out of here. She's our first priority. We'll be removing her through the window to the outside where a medical team is waiting for her. They have a special ambulance equipped with scanning machines. The hospital will know exactly what injuries they are dealing with before she gets to them. She'll be med evacuated out of here as soon as possible."

Sam nodded as he listened to the instructions. "I want to be kept informed of her condition if she has to leave here without me."

"You bet we'll keep you informed. The important thing for you to do is stay here and talk Ray through this. We need you to stay right here, Sam."

"Okay, you got it." Sam looked over at Ray and asked, "Did you hear all of that? I'm going to stay here with you, Ray. I'm sure they'll get you out of here as soon as they can. They're going to get Carly out first because she badly needs medical attention."

Ray nodded his head in agreement. "I don't know how much longer I can stand here, Sam. My knees are feeling like jelly."

"Stay with me, Ray. Tell me more about that baby of yours."

"Oliver," Ray smiled and relaxed a bit. "So Angie goes and paints the baby's room pink and then she finds out she's having a boy." He looked at Sam and stifled some tears. "She didn't mind, though. She was happy to go shopping all over again and get everything for a boy. Those were happy times for us."

Sam listened and nodded his head. He saw movement at the window behind Carly and watched as a man climbed onto the open windowsill and leaned over to pull Carly up. The chair made the removal awkward but after careful maneuvering Carly disappeared out the window. Sam let out a sigh of relief and wished he could be with her. He knew he was needed on the job and respected that duty as long as they stayed true to their promise to keep him updated on her condition.

"Okay everyone, we're going to wait until Carly has been cleared of the area and then we will proceed. We don't want to rush anything. It is important that we take our time and do this right."

Sam turned to Ray to get him talking again, "We had two girls and a boy. Now we have three grandchildren. Our youngest is now three months old. There's nothing better than that first smile."

"Oh yeah. Oliver isn't smiling yet. I can't wait until he does." He paused and looked down at his feet. "Maybe I won't get to see him smile."

"Tell me how things went at the hospital. Did everything go okay? Did you get to cut the cord? I got to cut the cord with our second and third baby. Not the first one, though. Our first one was a bit of an emergency and I couldn't do it then."

"Angie had a c-section. I passed out so Angie's mom was with her for the birth."

"You passed out? Aww, man. Sorry to hear that."

"As soon as I see blood I'm out. It doesn't affect me on the job though. I guess it's only with my own wife or something. You know, when it's personal and not some jerk that deserved what he got."

"All right, guys," the suited EOD tech came toward them. "We're going to need your cooperation. I'm going to put a rod on the trigger the same weight as Ray here. When I say it's okay, I want you to run down those stairs as fast as you can. If I do this right you'll have plenty of time to make your swift exit. Then I'm going to put a weighted bomb box over it to contain the explosion if it goes off." He looked at Sam and then at Ray. "Capiche?"

"Yeah, I can do that." Ray nodded his head. He made the sign of a cross and looked up heavenward and mouthed a silent prayer.

"I want that dog to make it out of here in one piece," Sam said putting his hand on the technicians arm. "I want the dog to come home with me."

"We're pretty sure we can get him out of here safe for you, Sam." The tech put the rod in place and adjusted the weight according to what Ray said was his weight. "On the count of three. One....Two.....Three!"

Ray stayed frozen in place so Sam grabbed him and hoisted him in a fireman carry and high tailed it out of there. He didn't stop until they were outside on the front lawn. The two men collapsed on the ground huffing and puffing.

Sam rolled over and caught sight of the med evac helicopter still parked there. He got up and looked around to find where they had Carly. He rushed over to where the ambulance was parked beside a tent to see his wife.

"She's in rough shape, Sam, but she's going to pull through." Ruthie put a hand on Sam's arm and leaned in to hug him. "I've been here waiting while they work on her. She's in good hands now. Her nose is busted, her left arm is busted, and probably a few broken ribs. With a little TLC she'll be good as new."

"I thought she'd be gone by now. Will they let me see her?"

"They're not letting anyone near her while they work on stabilizing her. From what I can tell she's on oxygen and they're hooking her up to an IV. They said I could fly with her to the hospital but now that you're here, it's better if you go with her."

"Where's Brett?"

"He's in there too. He'll be taken to the local hospital by ambulance but he's going to be okay. His face is a mess and probably some broken ribs but he'll recover in time." Ruthie chuckled. "You shoulda seen him pullin' one over on that ol' Campbell. Brett's one tough son of a gun." She put her hands up as though she was having an imaginary boxing match. "He was doin' pretty good too but then I had to shoot Campbell. He pulled out a gun and I had to put a stop to that."

"Were you the sniper that got Monique too?"

"The one and only. Not too shabby a job if I do say so myself."

"What would I do without you, Ruthie?"

"All in a day's work, Sam. I'm jes glad I could help out."

They watched as Brett was taken to the ambulance. Sam and Ruthie rushed over to talk to him before he left.

"Hey Brett," Sam edged his way closer. "You did good, buddy. Mission accomplished."

"How's Carly? She going to be okay?"

"Sure she'll be fine. I'm going to ride on the helicopter with her. We got her out of there alive and that's the best outcome of this whole mission. Not to mention that you are okay."

"I kept Campbell busy so the snipers could get him for us."

"You sure did. I heard you were like a professional UFC fighter out there. I must remember not to get you mad at me." Sam chuckled. "Seriously, though. You take it easy and do what those doctors tell you to do so you can get better."

"You come to my place, Brett. Ruthie'll take care of you. Me an' Walter'll wait on you hand and foot and get you back to your old self good as new."

"Thanks, Ruthie." Brett grabbed her hand. "Was that your fancy work that brought Campbell down?"

"You bet it was." Her grin lit up her whole face. "I take care of the people I care about when times are tough."

"Thanks for that." Brett waved as they loaded him into the ambulance and closed the doors.

Chapter 39

Reconnaissance Mission Successful

They loaded the stretcher onto the helicopter to take Carly to the hospital. The entire team watched. All faces were battered and weary but feeling pretty pleased to have pulled the mission off. They retrieved Mrs. Davenport and brought her back alive. There were moments when they doubted they could do that.

Sam gave them all a silent nod as they stood there. His approval meant a lot to them. They couldn't have asked for a better team commander. They worked together as a solid unit, like a well-oiled machine. This mission took all they had and they wouldn't have given any less than their best efforts.

The helicopter doors closed with Sam on board to be with his wife. She was in bad shape but she was alive. They watched the helicopter fly out of sight and then they turned to make their way back to normal life. No more crazy terrorists making threats and torturing innocent hostages. They would all end up in a bar somewhere together to drink and chill.

****

The patient lying on the stretcher did not look like his wife. She was unconscious, covered with bruises, bleeding and swelling. Sam sat back out of the way while they fussed over Carly. He wondered if she would ever forgive him. He felt responsible and he was ready for her anger. He saw her open her eyes and look around. "I'm here darling. Everything is going to be all right now. We're on the way to the hospital. The doctors will get you all fixed up." The tears were flowing from Sam's eyes and he wasn't ashamed. He was just so happy to see her wake up.

"Sam, it's you. Oh how I've missed you."

"I know, darling. I've missed you too. I'm just so glad we got you out of there."

"Is Brett going to be OK?"

"Yes, they patched him up just fine. You'd hardly notice a scratch on him. Well, other than his eye that's swollen shut."

"That poor man."

"He really fought for you, honey. He felt so bad that you were taken when he was in charge of seeing that no harm came to you. He was my right hand man through all of this. I owe him a debt of gratitude."

"Thank you for coming back for me, Sam."
"I could not be anywhere else. When my Carly was in danger I had to rescue her. You mean the world to me and I couldn't imagine my life without you."

"Oh Sam! Why did you lie to me about going to Las Vegas? You never retired from the military."

"Hey there, don't upset yourself. I have a lot of work ahead of me to gain your trust again. I did you wrong big time. What can I do to make it up to you?"

"Just hold my hand. I've wanted to hold your hand for such a long time. I feel safe now that you are here. I'll hit you later when I have enough strength back. It'll make me feel better. Then I'm never letting you out of my sight ever again."

****

Bouquets of pink roses, balloons of all shapes and sizes, and children's drawings filled the private hospital room where Carly sat on the edge of the bed. Sam helped her get into the wheelchair.

"I can't wait to get home, finally. Is it going to happen for real this time, Sam?"

"You bet it is. The kids are all waiting for us at the house. We're going to put you straight to bed when we get there. Curtis gets first pick of movies to watch and you'll never guess which one he picked."

"Oh let me guess, Toy Wars?"

"Wrong! He heard that you really liked to watch Gone With The Wind so he insisted I go out and buy it so we can all watch it together."

"Aww that's so sweet. I love that little guy."

"That's only part of it, I'm afraid. He plans to set up his trains and tracks all over your room because he doesn't want his Grandma to be bored while she's recuperating."

"That sounds heavenly to me. I want everyone around me as much as possible. I don't want to be alone for a long time. I look forward to having Claire read stories to me and I look forward to watching you change the baby's diapers."

"I'll do whatever it takes to make you happy, honey. You'll be happy to hear that I have officially retired from the military. It's for good this time. When you are feeling better we are going to go on a real holiday. You name the place and that's where we'll go."

"One question, honey." Carly looked up into Sam's eyes and asked, "You didn't really buy that airplane. Did you?"

"No, that was just a story to get you out of the house and away from danger. I'll never lie to you again. You can bet on that!"

When they arrived at the house, Sam parked in front of the house and helped Carly out. She walked gingerly to the front door and waited for Sam to unlock the door. They went inside and were bombarded by the kids and grandkids. Everyone was talking at once while they hugged and kissed.

"Grandma," Curtis called out. "We got chocolate muffins. Hurry so we can eat them. We're going to put up your Christmas tree too!"

"Oh darling, that sounds wonderful. I'm so hungry and I can't wait to try one."

Sam carried Carly up the stairs to the bedroom and placed her gently on the bed. Everyone crowded into the room. They all had some wild stories to share.

"Welcome home, Mom." Emma gave her mother a gentle hug. "We are going to come over every day to help Dad take care of you. The kids have everything all planned."

"I am going to read to you," said eight year old Claire. "We are going to clean the house for you too. Today is Wacky Wipe Wednesday. We have wet wipes and we are going to start with the doorknobs. Me and Curtis are going to wipe every doorknob in the house so there won't be any germs to make you sick."

Curtis climbed onto the bed and handed a chocolate muffin to Carly. "Here Grandma, you can have your muffin now so you don't have to be hungry no more."

"Thank you, Curtis. Can you help me out and take the wrapper off mine."

Sam handed a device to Carly. "The Dave crew sent you the neatest present, honey. It's a remote control for the baby's play pen. They set up a music mobile with music, a projector that displays pictures on the ceiling, and a mechanical teddy bear. All you have to do is push the buttons on the remote control and you can entertain the baby from your bed. You know, just in case I can't get to the baby on time and he starts to cry."

"Don't worry, mom, we'll all be here with you. We won't leave you alone to babysit Cooper."

"Grandma, Grandma! We will play games with you and watch movies. Did you play games and watch movies when you was a kid?" Curtis finished peeling the paper off the muffin and handed it to Carly.

Chapter 40

Surprise Plane Ride

They climbed out of the truck and Sam said, "I have a surprise for you, honey. We're going for a plane ride and I think you'll enjoy it much better this time."

They walked through the passenger entrance of the hanger in broad daylight this time. The Dave crew, once again dressed in their dirty old coveralls, was waiting for them. Dave H offered her a bottle of champagne complete with a red velvet bow. "This is for your flight," he said with a grin. "Enjoy it."

"Thanks! You guys are so great!" She gave each of the five Dave's a hug. "You know I was a little mad at first, but you made up for it. I'm glad to be here!" Carly looked serious. "I can never thank you all enough for everything you did for me."

Sam tugged Carly's hand towards the back of the hanger where the red carpet was laid out for them. It took them to the steps of the airplane. The pilot met them inside the door and handed a bouquet of pink roses to Carly. "These are for you ma'am. A gift from the entire staff. We hope you enjoy the flight."

"This time it's just me and you on the airplane, hon."

"You aren't going to fly the plane this time?" Carly asked.

"Nope. I'm just a passenger traveling with his beautiful wife. The only thing on the agenda is rest and relaxation."

"I like the sound of that," Carly said as she climbed into a seat. "Exactly how much does an airplane like this cost?"

"These babies cost about $5 million if you get it used and on sale. This particular airplane has military modifications thanks to the

Dave crew which would put it way up there in the priceless range."

"You really picked a doozie of a story to tell me to whisk me away from danger."

"Yeah, I'm sorry about that. My military duties have always required secrecy. From now on there won't be any reason to keep secrets from you. I'm about to be a retired man with nothing better to do than hang around the house and drive you crazy."

"Oh you won't be without something to do. I have a lot of projects I want you to do around the house."

They sat back in their seats and held hands during takeoff. Carly said a silent prayer and crossed herself like she always did. She watched out the window as they got higher and higher. It always amazed her that such a heavy airplane could get off the ground.

"This is where the trip gets more interesting," Sam said. "I have been reading up on the rules for joining the Mile High Club. It says two people must engage in sexual intercourse at an altitude of no less than 5,280 feet, which is a mile high above the earth, in an airplane. I'm all for it, how about you?"

Carly giggled. "Can we really do that? I mean won't the pilots know?"

"Aww heck, they have a do not disturb sign on their door. They won't be disturbing us. We have complete privacy. This trip was specially arranged for you and me. We'll do what comes natural a mile above the earth."

"Oh Sam, I love you!"

"Yeah, I'm a pretty good guy."

The two of them giggled as they removed clothing and got down to business.

****

An announcement came over the intercom. "There's a disturbance on the ground. It appears to be an international situation. There are hostages and some well known thugs. Headquarters is asking if you can take the case, Sam."

Carly and Sam looked at each other and began getting dressed. "I'm not retired yet, Carly. I promise this will be the last case."

It was stressful for Carly to watch her husband jump out of the airplane with a parachute on his back. She had never seen him do that before. She sat staring out the window for a long time watching his parachute float to the ground below. It amazed her to think that she had gone from ordinary housewife to the wife of a secret agent in a short time. Never in her wildest dreams had she imagined she'd ever become a full fledged member of the Mile High Club. She planned to enjoy that achievement for a very long time.

"Mrs. Davenport," the co-pilot stood looking at her. "Where would you like us to take you? Sam made us promise to take you somewhere safe out of harm's way."

Carly thought for a moment and heaved a heavy sigh. "Take me to Summerview Island. I promised to make a triple chocolate cheese cake for Ruthie and Walter. It will be nice to see them again. Can you call ahead and let them know I'm on my way?"

****

The taxi came to a stop in front of the porch. Carly paid the fare and climbed out of the back seat. She had no luggage once again but she would enjoy herself shopping for the things she needed later. She looked around the yard and made a mental note to pick up some pots of flowers to spruce the place up a bit.

The front door opened and a golden lab dog came rushing out

ahead of Ruthie. Walter followed behind them. Carly kneeled down to pet the dog when he came to her.

"That there's Major. We named him that on accounta we don't know what his real name is."

"He's beautiful. He's the dog that Sam's been talking about. I don't remember much about him but he seems to remember me."

"Yes he is a very friendly guy. Someone took a lot of time to teach him tricks too. A dog like that deserves to be with people that care about him. Not with crazy folks like that Monique and Campbell couple." Walter leaned in to give Carly a pat on the back. "Don't you go getting' no ideas about takin' him away from here. He's our baby now. We couldn't part with him no how."

"Don't worry, Walter. I won't take him away from you. He seems to be perfectly at home right here with you." Carly stood up and admired the way the dog went straight to Walter's feet and sat down. "He did his duty of greeting the newcomer and then he went right back to you. I can see who he considers his master."

"He likes Ruthie too. We discovered some of his tricks. He can play fetch an' he rolls over an' he shakes a paw." Walter leaned down to scratch Major's ear. "He keeps us old folks company so we's not all alone."

"You shoulda seen that dog when Brett was here recovering." Ruthie leaned down to pet Major. "Them two were never apart. Major here is a charmer an he's like a doctor dog or somethin'. Then when Brett went off to help Sam with this new mission, the dog cried till you got here!"

"So how you feeling?" asked Ruthie. "You look a might better'n the last time I laid eyes on you all bundled up on that there helicopter."

"I am on the mend, that's for sure. I wouldn't want to ever go through that again. If I ever have to face horrible people like that again I intend to be a little more up on my self defense."

"I can help ya with that if'n you want to," said Ruthie. "I can teach you how to shoot a gun."

"If you had offered that a month ago I would have declined the offer. However, it sounds pretty good to me after everything I went through. You point me in the direction of that rifle range and I'll practice with everything I got."

"How 'bout I teach you a little somethin' 'bout making bombs."

"Actually, I don't think I'm up to making bombs just yet, Walter. Thanks for the offer, though."

"Well shoot. I wanna help you with something too."

"Not a problem, my dear man." Carly put her arm around him as they walked into the living room. "You just sit down in your easy chair and watch some TV. I'm going to whip up a triple chocolate cheesecake. Then you can help me out by eating it and letting me know if it turned out okay."

"I can do that," Walter rubbed his hands together and licked his lips. "Cheesecake sounds perty good right now. Major can't have any on accounta dogs not being able to eat chocolate."

"I'll have to find something that Major can have. You all have me while Sam's on his newest mission and I have time on my hands to take care of you." Carly went to the kitchen and pulled out an apron and put it on. "Any special requests?"

"Roast chicken," Walter said. "With them little potaters. I like 'em roasted in the oven all crispy like and then load 'em up with ketchup."

"I'll check the freezer to see what supplies we have. I'll go shopping first thing tomorrow morning." Carly turned to Ruthie and asked, "You driving me to town tomorrow or can I borrow your car?"

"I'll be drivin' you. Ain't nobody runnin' off with you this time."

The End

Printed in Great Britain
by Amazon.co.uk, Ltd.,
Marston Gate.